THE CASE OF THE
ROCK 'N' ROLL DOG

MARTHA FREEMAN

Holiday House / New York

HOLIDAY HOUSE is registered in the U.S. Patent and Trademark Office.
Printed and bound in May 2010 at Maple Vail, York, PA, USA.
First Edition
1 3 5 7 9 10 8 6 4 2
www.holidayhouse.com

Library of Congress Cataloging-in-Publication Data
Freeman, Martha, 1956-
The case of the rock 'n' roll dog / Martha Freeman. — 1st ed.
p. cm.
Summary: Seven-year-old Tessa and ten-year-old Cameron,
daughters of the first female president—and owners of a very
rambunctious dog—play detective when a baton belonging to the director
of the Marine Band goes missing at the White House.
ISBN 978-0-8234-2267-8 (hardcover)
1. White House (Washington, D.C.)—Juvenile fiction.
[1. White House (Washington, D.C.)—Fiction.
2. Presidents—Family—Fiction. 3. Sisters—Fiction. 4. Dogs—Fiction.
5. Mystery and detective stories.]
I. Title. II. Title: Case of the rock and roll dog.
PZ7.F87496Cas 2010
[Fic]—dc22
2010011600

For my own first kids,
Sylvie, Rosa and
Ethan

CHAPTER ONE

SOMETIMES I wish Mom had lost the election and I had never been forced to leave my real life.

Monday was like that.

At school, my friend Kyle said Mom's hair looked frizzy when he saw her on CNN. And Andrea said since my mom's the president, can't she make a law so dogs don't chase cats? Then it was my teacher Ms. Nicols' turn. She said teachers should make more money, and she was looking at me when she said it.

So far so bad . . . and then we got our spelling tests back.

Spelling is not my best subject.

I mean, isn't it weird the way you spell *w-e-i-r-d*? And who put that extra *a* in *b-r-e-a-k-f-a-s-t?*

After school, the van picked us up to take us home to the White House. As usual, there was Nate, me and Tessa. That day Courtney came along, too.

Nate is my cousin who lives with us. Tessa is my little sister. And Courtney is my friend. She and I and Nate are all in fifth grade. We were going home together to work on reports.

When your mom's the president, you can't ride the school bus or walk or drive with a relative the way other kids do. You have to go in a special Secret Service van. Usually, either my aunt or my grandmother comes along. Today it was Aunt Jen's turn. Aunt Jen is my mom's sister and also Nate's mom.

"I have some news I think you're going to like," Aunt Jen said when our seat belts were buckled. "The Song Boys are coming to the White House."

Tessa, Courtney and I squealed.

Nate snorted. "The Song Boys are total bubblegum."

Tessa crossed her arms over her chest. "Like there's something bad about bubblegum?"

I laughed. Nate always acts *so superior*, but for once it wasn't worth it to be annoyed. I was too happy.

The Song Boys, in case you don't know, are the best boy band in America. They used to be three ordinary brothers—Jacob, Paul, and Matthew Song—who sang in the kids' choir at their church. Then a few years ago, their pastor put up on the Web a video of them singing "Michael, Row the Boat Ashore," and it got like a billion hits because at the end Matthew sticks his pinky finger up his nose.

That video still cracks me up.

Anyway, after that The Song Boys took music lessons and got the right clothes and their own TV show. I have every one of their songs and so do all my friends. At lunch we argue about which Song Boy is best.

In my opinion, Jacob and Matthew are fine, but Paul is better. He's the serious one. I have never met him, but if he called and asked me to marry him, I would say yes—as long as he waits for me to finish law school.

Since January when my mom became president, I have met a prince, the prime minister of England, two movie stars, and an opera singer. But if I get to meet Paul Song, I will probably faint.

"When are The Song Boys coming?" Tessa wanted to know. "Do I get to get dressed up?"

Aunt Jen said, "Saturday. And yes, you do, Tessa. It was all arranged in a hurry. The Song Boys had a concert date cancel."

"Uh . . . could I maybe be invited?" Courtney asked.

"We'll see," Aunt Jen said. "It's in the East Room so space will be limited. And the purpose is to promote literacy, so a lot of the guests will be librarians and teachers."

Courtney frowned, and I knew why. She thinks that Aunt Jen doesn't like her on account of her father, Alan Lozana. He used to be a TV reporter. Now he has this blog about politics. Usually what he writes about Mom isn't nice.

Both Aunt Jen and my dad get annoyed with Alan Lozana.

But Mom says: "If you can't stand the heat, stay out of the kitchen."

That means you better not be president if you mind what people say.

"What's 'promote literacy'?" Tessa asked.

"Getting people to read more," Aunt Jen explained.

My little sister can be a drama queen. Now she waved both hands the way she does. "*So why not just say that?!*"

The van always enters the White House grounds at the West Gate, and the driver stops to let the officer take a look inside and say hello. Then we pull up to the South Portico, get out, and go in through the Diplomatic Reception Room, called the Dip Room, which is on the ground floor. From there, we cross the hallway and either go up a spiral staircase or take the presidential elevator to the second floor.

That day Granny met us in the Dip Room, Aunt Jen went back to her office, and we took the elevator.

"Hi, Mr. Bryant," Nate said when the doors opened. The presidential elevator isn't automatic like other ones. It needs somebody inside to work it. That's Mr. Bryant. He is bald with a fringe of white hair. He says he has worked in the same elevator since Washington was president.

I know that's only a joke, though.

George Washington never even lived in the White House.

Mr. Bryant counted his passengers, "One, two,

three, four . . . five?" He squinted at Courtney through his glasses. "I don't believe I've had the pleasure."

Courtney held out her hand. "I've been here before, sir," she said.

Mr. Bryant shook his head. "My apologies, dear. The old peepers aren't what they used to be."

"What's a peeper?" Tessa asked.

"Eyes, *duh!*" Nate said.

"Duh yourself," Tessa said, and she probably would have said more, but Granny was right there.

"Going up," Mr. Bryant said, and the doors closed.

"Do you have new pictures?" Tessa asked.

Mr. Bryant pulled out his wallet. Inside were photos of two fluffy puppies. Mr. Bryant loves dogs.

Tessa said, "They're growing!"

Mr. Bryant said, "They should be. They eat like nobody's business."

"Did you know The Song Boys are coming?" Tessa asked him.

"I had heard something about that, yes," Mr. Bryant said. "Will the music be awfully loud, do you think?"

"I hope so!" Tessa said.

Mr. Bryant cringed, then said, "Second floor." He opened the doors for us. Hooligan must have heard the elevator coming because he was right there waiting.

"*Puppy*!" Tessa fell all over him with hugs.

"Not exactly a puppy, Tessa," Granny said. "More of a teenager—which explains a lot."

Hooligan is big and skinny with too-long legs and a too-long tail. He also has too much energy, which is why—even though he really tries to be good—he gets into so much trouble. In fact, he's a lot like the dog in "Rock'n'Roll Dog," which just happens to be his very favorite Song Boys song.

Now he trotted along with us to the family kitchen for our after-school snack: cookies, milk and something healthy. The cookies come from a special small kitchen between the first and second floors of the White House. When we moved here in the winter, we ate cookies all the time. Then Mom decided so many aren't good for us. And now we're only allowed one each after school.

Sometimes I dream of cookies.

Today's were snickerdoodles, which are sugar with cinnamon. I took a bite. *Yummy.* My bad day had gotten a whole lot better. But then Nate pulled his spelling test out of his backpack to show Granny. He had a perfect score. And Granny turned to me. "Didn't you get yours back, too, Cameron?"

CHAPTER TWO

WHEN Granny saw all the marks on my spelling test, she said we could practice on the way to school.

Then, when she wasn't looking, Nate stuck out his tongue at me.

Sometimes I hate my cousin.

If you're wondering why he lives with us, it's because when my mom was elected there was no one to be First Lady. I mean, no offense to my dad, but he would never make it as First Lady. Besides, during the week he has a job in California building airplanes. Most of the time, we only see him on weekends.

Anyway, just like my mom asked her own mom to take care of me and Tessa, she asked her little sister, Jen, to move from San Diego and be "White House Hostess."

The news guys call her "First Auntie."

I like Aunt Jen so that part was okay. Unfortunately, Nate came along in the deal.

Besides being good at spelling, Nate is some kind

of piano genius, and he is tall and gets good grades. Some people (like my mother!!!) say he's handsome, too.

I don't think he likes me and Tessa very much.

Granny says Tessa and I are too hard on Nate. She says it's tough to be the new kid and besides Nate is shy. I say the real problem is how Nate acts so superior all the time.

The something healthy part of our snack that day was apples, carrots and celery. When we were done eating, Courtney, Nate and I went up to the solarium. It's at the top of the White House, and it's like our family room—with the TV and the Ping-Pong table and a view of the Washington Monument.

Tessa and Hooligan came, too. Tessa's in second grade. She didn't have homework. But we were taking all the markers, and she wanted to draw pictures of outfits.

Upstairs, we kids settled in on the floor to work, and Hooligan settled in on the floor to nap.

Our assignment was to write and illustrate a report about a famous American. My famous American was Sandra Day O'Connor—the first woman justice on the Supreme Court.

Courtney's was Nellie Bly, a reporter from more than a hundred years ago.

Nate's was John Philip Sousa, a musician and

composer who wrote marches like "Stars and Stripes Forever."

You might not think you know that song, but I bet you do. Somebody wrote silly words for it: "Be kind to your web-footed friends, for that duck may be somebody's mo-o-other. . . ."

See, you do know it, right?

We had done most of the writing part of our reports in class, so now we were illustrating. My picture was Sandra Day O'Connor's ranch in Arizona. I started to draw a cactus.

Courtney was drawing something called a typewriter that looks like a computer keyboard.

Nate was drawing a fat brown line.

Nate is not a very good artist, but still. A fat brown line?

He saw me looking.

"I'm drawing John Philip Sousa's baton," he explained.

Tessa looked over. "Was John Philip Who-za a baton twirler, too?"

It wasn't that funny. But Nate laughed like he would bust a gut. When he finally stopped, I said, "Not that kind of baton, Tessa. The same word means the stick a band director uses."

"And it's Sousa, not Who-za!" Nate started laughing all over again.

Tessa narrowed her eyes at him. "What*ev*er," she said.

Nate can never resist telling everything he knows.

"The Sousa baton is special," he said. "John Philip Sousa used to be the director of the Marine Band. In 1892, when he retired, they gave him this baton. After he died, the baton was donated back to the band by his family. The book I read says the Marine Band director still uses it today. In fact, there's a tradition that the band can't play without it!"

All this time, Hooligan had been napping on the floor next to us. Now, for mysterious doggie reasons, his eyes blinked open.

Hooligan doesn't wake up slow and groggy like me. He wakes up ready to rock'n'roll!

"Watch your markers," I said. "Hooligan thinks they're chew toys."

Courtney said, "He can't have mine!" and made a sudden move to corral them.

This was a mistake.

Sudden moves are specialties of squirrels, chipmunks and rabbits. Hooligan loves squirrels, chipmunks and rabbits. He thinks they're chew toys, too.

Now our dog was not only wide awake, he was excited. And sometimes when he's excited, he does this thing we call the *frenzy*: He lunges forward, thumps his paws, springs high in the air, then spins so fast he turns blurry.

You can never tell for sure when he's going to do it, but if he does—*blam-o!*

Tessa knew the signs. "Uh-oh." She grabbed for his collar . . . but it was too late!

Hooligan lunged, thumped, sprang and spun—this time with an extra added marker grab in the middle.

I thought the grab was a nice touch; Courtney was not a fan. "*No!*" she squealed, which Hooligan heard as: "*Let's play!*" There was a fast tug of war. Courtney lost. Then Hooligan sprinted off with three markers in his fearsome jaws.

Nate stayed put, but Courtney, Tessa and I chased Hooligan once around the solarium then down the ramp that leads to the floor below. Two markers fell, but he kept the pink one. We know it was pink because every once in a while he bumped the wall and it left a stripe. Finally, we rounded a corner, and he was gone.

"What happened to him?" Courtney was breathing hard.

I shook my head. "He's been disappearing a lot lately—going AWOL my dad calls it."

There are six floors in the White House, and 132 rooms not counting all the offices, storage rooms and workspaces. It's not that hard to hide, even for a too-big dog.

"Hoo-hoo-hooligan!" Tessa's holler was a yodel. "Hoo-hoo-hooligan—*fetch!*"

Hooligan is not exactly well trained. Tell him to sit, stay or heel, and you might as well be speaking Cat. But *fetch* he understands. You never know what he'll fetch or where—but some kind of fetch will happen.

Courtney shook her head, disgusted. "My dog Rex *never* behaves this way."

Tessa said Courtney's dog Rex was about as fun as a sofa cushion.

Courtney told her to take it back.

Tessa said she wouldn't—and this could have gone on a while except here came the sound of galloping doggie toenails, and a second later Hooligan appeared at the end of the hallway, bounding toward us at top speed.

There was something in his mouth—something bigger than a marker.

I sidestepped the same way I'd sidestep a soccer defender.

But Courtney takes tap not soccer, and—*blam!* Hooligan caught her in the knees. Then—*ooof!* Down she went.

At least the rug was soft.

Courtney lay on the floor as if she were dead. "Are you okay?" I asked.

"I hate your dog," she said.

"What hurts? Do you need a Band-Aid?" Tessa asked.

Courtney opened her eyes. "Everything hurts! Do you have a whole-body Band-Aid?"

I reached down and helped Courtney up. She didn't look that bad—except for the big, fat frown on her face.

Back in the solarium, Hooligan was sitting on his haunches, thumping his tail and smiling a big doggie smile at Nate. He was hoping for a dog yummy—since he'd done such a great job at fetch. But he hadn't brought back the pink marker. He'd brought Skateboard Barbie.

No way would Nate touch a Barbie, so it was Tessa who rescued her. When Hooligan didn't go crazy or fight her for it, I knew he was tired out, too.

Tessa did a quick inspection. "No teeth marks on her face at least."

"You *told* him to fetch," I reminded her.

"I want my marker back," Courtney said.

"At least he didn't eat our homework," I said.

CHAPTER THREE

BESIDES being my best friend, Courtney is also my worst enemy.

Maybe you know what I mean?

If you don't, I will explain. A best friend and worst enemy is a person you can't live without because you have known her so long. And it's a person you can't live with because she annoys you so much.

Courtney has been my friend since we were three year olds in preschool. That's when Mom was elected to be a senator from California, and we moved to Washington, D.C.

Back when Mom was a plain senator, Courtney's dad didn't write about her much, but now he writes about her a lot. This is a problem, and there's another one besides. I can tell sometimes Courtney feels jealous about how I live in the White House.

She doesn't get that it's not all wonderful.

I mean, there *are* good parts. Like riding in the helicopter. And I don't have to do chores like washing dishes. But we fold our own clothes and make our own beds because Granny doesn't want us to think we're some kind of special.

Our other chore is taking care of Hooligan. We feed him and take turns cleaning out his dog bed—sweeping the basket and the cushion, shaking out the blanket, spraying away doggie smell.

This is a pretty gross job, though, and sometimes by mistake we both forget.

Even the good parts of life in the White House come with problems. Like with The Song Boys. I couldn't wait for their concert! But I was also worried about Courtney. She was going to be so mad if she wasn't invited.

Then on Tuesday, I found out I should have been even *more* worried. By the time I got to school, everyone in my class knew The Song Boys were coming.

And guess what? They expected to be invited, too!

I told Granny after school, and she said, "There's only one thing to do. Talk to Aunt Jen."

Granny is Aunt Jen's mom, but even Granny is a little afraid of her. It's not that Aunt Jen's mean. It's just that she's not exactly cozy.

Aunt Jen's office is in the East Wing. Nate and Tessa and I are allowed to go anywhere in the family part of the White House by ourselves. But if we want to go to the office part, someone has to come with us. Today it was Charlotte. She is my favorite Secret Service agent.

To get to the East Wing, you go down two floors

and then through a long hallway past a fancy library and a real movie theater with red velvet seats and paintings of First Ladies from a long time ago. The best one is named Mamie Eisenhower. She has bangs and a kind smile. She is wearing a beautiful light pink dress.

While we walked, I told Charlotte why I had to see Aunt Jen.

"I feel your pain, kid," she said. "My friends ask me for White House favors, too."

"What favors?" I asked.

She grinned. "Well, one of my nieces wanted a signed picture of you and Tessa, just for example."

"I probably have a picture someplace," I said.

Charlotte shook her head. "You know your family's not into that, Cameron. They want you to act like kids, not movie stars. Here we are."

Aunt Jen's secretary, Mrs. Crowe, smiled and said we could go right in.

In Aunt Jen's office, I explained, and she sighed. "How many people do you want to invite?" she asked.

I looked at my shoes.

"Oh dear," she said. "Your whole class?"

I nodded.

"Including Courtney Lozana?"

"Especially Courtney Lozana," I said.

Aunt Jen shook her head. "It's awfully tight for the security clearances," she said, "but I'll talk to Mrs. Silver, and we'll see what we can do."

Mrs. Silver is the White House social secretary. She works for my aunt, and her job is planning parties and events like The Song Boys.

I told Aunt Jen thank you, and I would have given her a hug, but she doesn't like to get wrinkled.

"You're welcome," she said. Then, as I was walking out the door, she asked me to hold on a minute. "Just do me one favor, Cameron. We'll let the class know all at once, and as soon as we can. In the meantime, please don't pester me about it. Do we have a deal?"

"We have a deal," I said.

Going back upstairs, I heard music from the state floor. Not random music either. A song I totally knew by heart, "Shake it Up!" from The Song Boys' second album. I felt a thump in my chest.

Were The Song Boys here already?!

"Not yet, kid," Charlotte said. "That's the Marine Band. They're going to play with the Boys on Saturday. Usually they'd rehearse at the barracks, but today they're trying out sound equipment."

When we got back upstairs, Granny, Nate and Tessa were in the West Sitting Hall. So was Hooligan—in his bed. When he saw me, he raised his head and thumped his tail, but he didn't get up.

"Hooligan's had a busy day," Granny said.

"Who did he knock over this time?" Nate asked.

"Very funny," said Granny, "and no one, I hope. But he did go AWOL for a while."

Even from up here, we could hear the music.

Granny had already explained to Tessa and Nate about the band. Tessa tugged on Granny's sleeve. "Can we go watch?"

Granny considered. "How much homework do you have?"

Tessa and I answered together: "Hardly any."

Nate said, "Cameron should study spelling."

My turn to stick my tongue out—and luckily Granny didn't see. She had closed her eyes to listen to the music—and next thing you know, she was rocking out!

Tessa and I high-fived and rocked out, too. Nate just stood there like a lump.

Still bouncing, Granny said, "It's catchy. Tell you what. We'll all go down and listen."

Nate crossed his arms. "Not me."

CHAPTER FOUR

FIVE minutes later we were standing in the East Room—Granny, Tessa, me and Nate. He should know it's no use arguing with Granny.

The East Room is on the state floor. It's as big as a basketball court—the biggest room in the White House. It's gold and white with three giant, sparkling chandeliers and four fireplaces. Sometimes, like now when there's going to be an event, it's mostly empty of furniture. Once a long time ago a kid named Amy Carter lived in the White House, and she even got to roller-skate in the East Room.

When we walked in, the musicians were between songs. Colonel Michaels, the director, looked up and saw us. "Good afternoon, children. Good afternoon, Judge Maclaren."

Granny is "Granny" to us, but she used to be a judge in California and before that a police officer.

"Good afternoon, Colonel Michaels," said Granny. "We've come to listen if you don't mind."

"Happy to have you." Colonel Michaels turned to face the band and raised his hands. But then he dropped them and looked around. A trumpet player held up a smooth, shiny wooden stick and handed it to Colonel Michaels.

"That's it," Nate whispered to me, "the Sousa baton!"

"It doesn't look that special," Tessa said.

"It's historic!" Nate said.

Colonel Michaels raised the baton and smiled. "I can't very well direct without this, can I?"

Nate nudged me. "See?"

Then the musicians raised their instruments, and . . . "A-*one*, anna *two*, anna one-two-three-*four* . . ."

The trumpets blared the first notes of another big Song Boys hit: "Praise a Ruckus."

The band's official name is the President's Own Marine Band. It has 160 members—men and women—but most of the time they don't all play together. For The Song Boys, it was going to be their chamber orchestra along with guitars and a drum set. This was a rehearsal, so the musicians wore plain brown uniforms and shiny black shoes.

I will never get to roller-skate in the East Room. But Granny does believe in dancing. She, Tessa and I had formed a conga line when Hooligan showed up in the doorway. Where did he come from anyway?

Of course, he should've been on a leash. But we were having too much fun to go upstairs and get it. Tessa even grabbed his front paws so the two of them could dance together.

The musicians took a short break, and then they played Hooligan's favorite, "Rock'n'Roll Dog."

How could he help but howl?

Granny looked at me and raised her eyebrows, the universal sign for: *Control your dog, Cameron.*

I bent down and lifted Hooligan's ear. *"Shhh!"*

Unfortunately, Hooligan misunderstood. He thought I said: *"Part-y-y-y!"* because he tensed his muscles, blinked twice, and did the frenzy—lunged, thumped, sprang and spun. Back on the ground for an instant, he looked left, looked right and took off like he had a squirrel to catch.

Next thing we knew, he was bounding toward the band and yipping in time with the music. At first, I thought everything would be all right. In fact, the way the Marines stepped and sidestepped to avoid him looked like MTV.

But then Hooligan's too-long tail brushed a music stand that hit the one next to it, and the next and the next, and then the cymbals on the drum set. . . .

The clatter was so terrible it even scared Hooligan, who jumped like he'd heard a starter's pistol. Next thing you know, people were running in from every direction to see what was the matter: Mr. Ross, the head usher; Mr. Baney, the florist; Mr. Patel, the handsome steward; a maid named Mrs. Hedges; and Mr. Kane, one of the chefs.

Mr. Ross is from Texas, and when he saw our rampaging dog, he must've thought of a rampaging cow because he hollered, "Round-up!"

Unfortunately, Hooligan is quicker than any cow, and anyway we didn't have lassos. Three times we had him surrounded, and three times he busted free.

That's when Granny's police training kicked in.

"Tessa," she ordered, "you go right. Cameron, take the door, and Nathan—you've got my back." As we scurried to position ourselves, Granny strode into the path of the oncoming Hooligan, raised her right hand and said, "Halt!"

Face to face with Granny, even a getaway car would stop.

But not my wild and crazy dog.

He scooted by on her right and almost took out Nate. That left me as the last defender between Hooligan and escape!

Have I mentioned the state floor of the White House is full of rare, historic and breakable antiques?

Hooligan was poised to take a mighty leap across the East Room threshold when I hurled my body forward and . . . *crash!* We collided, then . . . *ow!* I hit the floor hard.

So did my dog.

After all the clattering, yelling and stomping, the room went suddenly still. Then in the silence I heard Tessa's voice: "Puppy! Poor puppy! Are you okay?"

And Colonel Michaels said, "I think that will conclude today's rehearsal."

CHAPTER FIVE

IT'S amazing how much damage one too-large dog can do—even in a room that's mostly empty.

The next few minutes were a whirlwind of activity as the staff tried to put the East Room back in order and the band packed up. I sat with Tessa in the middle of it all, holding Hooligan firmly by the collar.

"Judge Maclaren, you don't have to help," Mr. Ross told Granny. She was on her knees, tugging the corner of a rug to flatten it out.

"Oh, yes I do." She explained she felt responsible because she should have insisted on getting Hooligan's leash.

Finally, the band was ready to leave, and Granny said, "I'll take the dog, girls. You go and apologize to Colonel Michaels."

"What about Nate?" Tessa asked.

Granny looked around. "I don't know where he's got to, but it doesn't matter. Hooligan is *your* dog."

Colonel Michaels is tall and serious with perfect

posture and a spotless uniform. Even though Tessa is only seven, I was glad she was standing next to me. I wouldn't have wanted to apologize alone.

"We're sorry about Hooligan," I said.

"He has too much energy," Tessa said.

"And it was his favorite song," I said.

"This is Hooligan's home, not ours," Colonel Michaels said. "But I do wish we'd been able to complete the rehearsal." He looked at his watch. "And now I'm afraid we're running late. See you on Saturday?"

"Yes, sir," we said at the same time.

"I look forward to it," said Colonel Michaels.

"Cammie?" Tessa said a minute later when we were walking up the stairs. "He didn't exactly forgive us, did he?"

"Not exactly," I said.

Upstairs, Hooligan flopped onto his bed and fell instantly asleep.

Then Nate appeared from the kitchen.

"Where did you go?" Granny asked him.

"Who me?" Nate said. "No place! Uh . . . I mean, I came back up here is all. . . ."

Granny cocked her head, then she looked at Tessa and me. "You still have some time before dinner. I think all three of you had better set yourselves down and do some schoolwork."

"Mine would be done except I had to listen to stupid music," Nate said.

Granny shut her eyes. "It will be in your best interest, Nathan, if I pretend I did not hear that last comment."

"Besides, I saw you tapping your feet!" Tessa said. "You just don't want to admit you like The Song Boys 'cause you think they're for kids. Well, *you're* a kid! Get over it!"

Nate crossed his arms. "I hate The Song Boys," he said, "and you know what else? I hope something bad happens, and they can't even play on Saturday."

Granny put her hands on her hips. "That is too much, Nathan. Apologize to your cousins."

"Sorry, cousins," Nate said—but in a robot voice so we would know he didn't mean it.

There are eleven bedrooms in the White House—plenty to go around—but Tessa and I still share. We were afraid it would be spooky to sleep alone in an old house. Our room is big, with two beds and two bookcases. My bookcase is full of books. Tessa's is full of Barbies.

That night, it was Mom who came in to say good night. Usually, we eat dinner with Granny because Mom is so busy being president. When she's in town, though, Mom always comes in to kiss us good night.

"I understand there was some uproar with Hooligan today." Mom was sitting on the edge of Tessa's bed. She wore gray sweats and a gray Stanford sweatshirt. In our family, it's Tessa and Aunt Jen who are into fashion. Mom and me—not so much.

"Hooligan is not the problem," Tessa told her. "Nate is the problem."

"Why do we have to live with him, Mom?" I asked.

"Shall I send him back to San Diego?" Mom asked.

"Yes!" Tessa and I said.

"What about Aunt Jen?" Mom said.

"She can stay," I said.

"Then who will Nate live with in San Diego?" Mom asked.

This was a problem. Aunt Jen's husband died in a war. It was later she adopted Nate. He was born in Korea. "Doesn't he have friends in San Diego?" I asked.

Mom nodded. "That's an idea. Or what about this? You girls could go live with friends, and Nate can stay here."

Tessa knew Mom didn't mean it. But she likes to be dramatic. "*No-o-o-o!*" She waved her hands. "We want to live with *you*—with our *family!*"

Mom smiled and gave her a kiss and a snuggle. Then she came over and gave me a kiss and a snuggle. Mom smelled like roses.

"You know what, muffins," she said. "I bet Nate feels the same way. I bet he wants to live with *his* family."

I was going to answer her. But I was sleepy. And when I'm sleepy, my mom is too smart for me.

CHAPTER SIX

THE next day was Wednesday, and before the first bell rang, Nate's and my teacher called me to her desk.

"There are a lot of rumors going around about The Song Boys, Cameron," she said. "Would you like a chance to address them?"

I said that depended on what "address them" meant.

Ms. Nicols smiled. "It means, would you like to tell everybody once and for all whether they are going to be invited?"

"But I don't know yet!" I said. "All Aunt Jen told me is she's doing her best."

"I see," Ms. Nicols said. "Well, it's up to you. But I'm afraid it's going to become a distraction if you don't say something."

I looked at my toes. "I guess I could say *something*."

"Good," Ms. Nicols said. "I'll call on you after the bulletin."

At first when I found out The Song Boys were coming, I thought it was the best thing that ever happened. Now it was more like the worst thing. I hate to talk in front of the class. And it doesn't help that people expect me to be good at it.

Just because my mom is good at something, does it mean I have to be?

I listened to the bulletin, wishing it would go on forever. But like always it ended after the cafeteria menu.

"And now, class," Ms. Nicols said, "Cameron wishes to address us. Cameron?"

Standing up, I heard a rude noise from a desk in back. Nate. At least I hoped so.

"Uh . . . so I know everybody's hoping they can come to the White House to see The Song Boys on Saturday . . . ," I started.

Nate interrupted: "Not me! I hate The Song Boys."

"Nathan?" Ms. Nicols said. "Could you let your cousin have her say, please?"

Now I was even more nervous. "Uh . . . but the thing is there's something called security clearances, and that's why—"

"Cameron?" Now Ms. Nicols interrupted. "Could you explain that, please? Not everyone has had the experience of living in the White House."

A couple of people giggled.

I took a deep breath, and then I said how a security clearance means the Secret Service makes sure people visiting the White House aren't planning to hurt anything.

"And it takes a while for the Secret Service to do that, and then if there's a problem, uh . . . well, that person can't come," I said. And then I sat down.

"Wait just a moment, Cameron. Is there a problem?"

Unhappily, I stood back up. At this rate Saturday would come and go with me still standing in front of the class. "I don't think so," I said. "But Aunt Jen told me not to bug her about it. She and Mrs. Silver will let everyone know at the same time—and she promises that will be as soon as possible."

Ms. Nicols thanked me and said—finally—I could sit back down. "So now I hope everyone's questions about Saturday are answered," she said brightly, "and we can move along with our day!"

Ms. Nicols may be the education professional, and I may be the ten-year-old. But even I knew "move-along-with-our-day" was not going to happen.

And it didn't.

I won't torture you with details. But maybe you have had a birthday party and your mom let you invite five people, and everybody was talking about who wasn't going? Or maybe you got the lunchbox or the music player or the bicycle everybody wanted, and now they're saying you're spoiled? Or maybe a friend decided he didn't like you anymore, and now his friends won't sit with you at lunch?

Well, pretend all those things happened on the same day, multiply that times a hundred, and add in one cousin who spends the whole day insulting your friends' taste in music. That's what Wednesday was like for me.

At three ten when we were packing our backpacks to go home, Courtney tried to make me feel better.

"I still like you, Cammie," she said. "And even if I don't get invited, I will still still like you."

"Thank you," I said.

"But," she added, "I'll like you better if I do get invited."

I wasn't looking forward to being trapped in the van with Nate all the way home. But it turned out not to matter. The second our seat belts were buckled, Granny said, "Hooligan is AWOL again, and Mr. Ross is not happy."

Like I said, Mr. Ross is the head usher. I know that sounds like a job in a theater, but actually he's in charge of the whole White House. The job got the name in the 1800s when the main thing that person had to do was usher people in to see the president.

"So this time," Granny continued, "I think we should apprehend the fugitive ourselves—if you don't have too much homework, that is."

"We don't!" we all said at the same time. And we spent the rest of the drive discussing what Granny calls logistics. In the end, we decided to search from top to bottom. So, after eating our single solitary cookies along with a bunch of grapes and some celery sticks, we deployed to the solarium.

The ground and state floors of the White House are the public parts. The family part is mostly on the second and third floors. Mom and Dad, and Tessa and I have our bedrooms on the second, while Aunt Jen and Nate's rooms are on the third. From the third floor, there is a ramp that leads up to the solarium.

"All right, troops," Granny said when we reached the top of the ramp. "It is now—" she looked at her watch "—sixteen fifteen hours. Cammie, you take the rooms north of the hall. Tessa, you're going south. Nathan—your job is to search up here in the kitchen and storage rooms. We reconvene at sixteen twenty-five. Is that clear?"

"Yes, ma'am!" we said.

"A-a-a-a-a-and *fan out!*"

The three of us ran back toward the hall. Nate went straight ahead. "Hoo-hoo-*hooligan!*" we yodeled. But the only answer was an echoing "Hoo-*hooligan!*"

Ten minutes later, we had looked under beds and tables and behind curtains and toilets, but there was not a snuffle or a whimper or a *scritch-scratch.*

"We now know for sure where Hooligan is *not*," Granny said. "I've done a pretty good search of the second floor myself, so let's go downstairs."

In the morning, the public can tour the state floor of the White House, so we stay out of the way. But in the afternoon there aren't tours, so we can come down if we want. I was looking under a sofa in the Blue Room when Tessa came running.

Something was wrong. Was Hooligan hurt?

"No, no, not *Hooligan*!" Tessa was out of breath. "The baton—the historic Who-za one Nate knows about? It's *missing*!"

CHAPTER SEVEN

"NOT Who-za—*Sousa!*" I said.

Tessa waved her arms. "What*ever.*"

Then she explained.

She had gone into the East Room looking for Hooligan and found Colonel Michaels. "He told me the baton is missing," Tessa said.

I said, "That's too bad," because I could see she was upset. But really, I was relieved nothing bad had happened to Hooligan.

Tessa shook her head. "You still don't get it, Cammie. It's not too bad. It's *really* bad! Without the baton, there's no Song Boys!"

"Why not?" I asked.

"The Marine Band can't play unless they have it. Nate said so. No band—no Song Boys."

Was this true? Or was this Tessa drama?

"Come on," I said. "We better talk to Colonel Michaels."

We found him in the East Room. Remembering

how he hadn't exactly forgiven us, I was extra polite. "Good afternoon, Colonel Michaels."

"Good afternoon, Cameron. I suppose your sister has explained?"

"It's becoming a real mystery!" Tessa said. "Cammie and I are good at solving mysteries. Dad asks us to find his missing glasses all the time."

"They are usually on his head," I said.

"Plus detecting skills run in our family," Tessa went on. "Granny used to be a cop."

"Police officer," I said.

"Well, I could certainly use the help of skilled detectives," said Colonel Michaels. "It's important that I get the baton back before Saturday. Otherwise, how will I keep the beat for The Song Boys?"

"We know all about your baton," Tessa said. "Nate wrote a report on John Philip—"

"—Sousa," I said before she could get it wrong.

"Did he now?" said Colonel Michaels. "And he mentioned the Sousa baton?"

Tessa nodded. "And how the band can't play without it."

Colonel Michaels shook his head. "Oh dear. That old myth."

"It isn't true?" I said.

"No, it's not," said Colonel Michaels. "Somewhere some author wrote that the Sousa baton is in regular use. And from there someone got the idea we don't perform without it. But the fact is the Sousa baton is so valuable it's only used for ceremonial occasions."

Ha! I thought. For once our *so superior* cousin got something wrong!

"Then what baton is it that's missing?" Tessa asked.

"My own, and I want it back," said Colonel Michaels. "Could I assign you two experienced detectives to solve the mystery?"

"Sure," I said.

"Sure!" Tessa said. "First, we have some questions."

I looked over at my sister. "We do?"

Tessa shrugged. "That's what they say in books."

"Go ahead," said Colonel Michaels.

Tessa crossed her arms over her chest. "Colonel Michaels," she said, "when did you last see the baton?"

"I had it yesterday when I was directing right here in this room," Colonel Michaels said. "Then there was the, uh . . . fracas with your dog, and we packed up in haste. I thought I had put the baton away as usual, but when I opened the case today, it was empty."

"We're sorry about Hooligan," I couldn't help saying.

"Yes," said Colonel Michaels. "I know. In fact, it occurred to me he might be the culprit. Dogs and sticks, you know. With all the excitement, I easily could have set it down for him to pick up."

"That was good thinking," Tessa said.

"Thank you," Colonel Michaels said. "Do you have more questions?"

"I don't think so," Tessa said. "What about you, Cammie?"

"Hooligan couldn't have taken the baton," I said.

"That's not a question," said Tessa.

"Oh, sorry. But he couldn't have. Everyone was watching when he went crazy, and after that we had him by the collar. Then Granny did. And then we took him upstairs. He never had a chance to steal anything."

Colonel Michaels nodded. "Yes, I see. Perhaps I was too quick to blame him."

"We'll find your baton, Colonel Michaels," Tessa assured him. "We'll even get Granny to help."

Colonel Michaels picked up his hat. "Thank you, girls. And good luck."

After that, it was time to go back upstairs. And guess where we found Hooligan?

In his bed—relaxing like he'd been there all day!

Tessa and I sat down on the floor beside him.

"Do you realize all the trouble you caused us?" she asked.

"Where were you, anyway?" I asked.

Hooligan looked up and thumped his tail. I think he wanted to tell us. But he couldn't woof the words.

CHAPTER EIGHT

MOST of the time, Nate eats with Tessa, me and Granny. But that night he was having dinner with Aunt Jen upstairs. They had something particular to talk about, Granny said. She wouldn't tell us what, but she did say the topic had nothing to do with San Diego.

Too bad.

Dinner was macaroni and cheese with applesauce and green salad. Usually our dinners come from the White House kitchen, and we eat in the family dining room on the second floor. On special occasions, we eat in the small dining room downstairs, and on *really* special occasions—like if an important queen or a movie director comes to visit—we might get to eat with everybody else in the State Dining Room.

While we ate, we told Granny about how we met up with Colonel Michaels in the East Room, and he asked us to find the missing baton. After that, we asked for detecting advice.

"I was never actually a detective, you know. I was

a beat cop and eventually a sergeant. Then I went to law school," Granny said.

"That's when Mom was little, right?" I asked.

"Aunt Jen was in preschool when I started," Granny said. "And your mom was in second grade like Tessa here. Your grandpa had been dead a couple of years."

"Why did you want to go to law school?" I asked.

Granny sat back in her chair. "Cops investigate crimes, but they can't put criminals in prison," she said. "That's what prosecutors do. And for that job, you have to be a lawyer. Then—I won't lie—money mattered. Most of the time, lawyers earn more than police officers. I had two little girls to raise."

"Even if you weren't a detective," Tessa said, "you must have seen mysteries get solved. Plus you saw how bad guys get caught."

"Wait a sec, Tessa. We don't even know if there *is* a bad guy," I said. "Probably, the baton is just lost."

Tessa frowned. "*That* wouldn't be very interesting."

Granny laughed. "In my experience, most criminals are tripped up by stupidity. Smart people find smarter things to do than commit crimes."

Tessa nodded thoughtfully. "So the first thing we should do," she said, "is look for somebody stupid."

"Well, detectives first look for anything strange or out of place because it might be a clue," Granny said. "Then, of course, they interview witnesses."

"We already interviewed Colonel Michaels," Tessa said.

"Excellent," Granny said. "Who else was a witness?"

"Everyone in the East Room yesterday afternoon," I said.

"That includes me," Granny said, "but I only saw the baton when it was in Colonel Michaels's hand."

I said I thought we should write a list of everybody who was there, then talk to as many as we could. "Does that make sense, Granny?"

"It does," she said. "But if you're planning on doing interviews tomorrow, you'll have to be quick about it. Your aunt has some kind of dinner going on. Oh, and be sure to take notes. Later, you look through your notes and—" she tapped her head with her finger "—apply logic."

"I'll take the notes because my handwriting is good," I told Tessa. "And you can do the talking because . . ." I hesitated.

"I'm a loudmouth!" Tessa grinned. "I knew someday that would come in handy."

After dinner, we wrote our list. We probably wouldn't be able to talk to the musicians, but we could talk to people from the staff who had been there. The ones we remembered were: Mr. Ross, Mr. Baney, Mr. Patel, Mrs. Hedges and Mr. Kane.

Mom had a meeting that went late, so it was Granny who came in to say good night. I was sinking into my pillow when there was a knock, and the door opened a crack.

"Are you awake?" Mom whispered.

"We didn't used to be," Tessa said.

Tonight Mom was dressed in her Madam President clothes—stockings, high heels, skirt and jacket. She came in and sat on the edge of Tessa's bed, but immediately bounced back up. "*Ow!* What was . . . ?" She held something up.

"Ski Barbie!" Tessa said. "Thanks for finding her, Mom."

"Hmmph," Mom said. "Those poles are sharp!" Then she apologized for coming in so late. "The senators are still arguing about that energy bill. If it goes much longer, I'll have to run up to Capitol Hill and knock heads together."

"Cool!" Tessa said. "Can I watch?"

Mom laughed. "I didn't mean it literally. I meant, uh . . . I'll have to offer some encouragement. Now, what did you girls do today?"

We told her about school and about how Hooligan went AWOL again. I was going to explain how Colonel Michaels had assigned us to find his baton, but by then it was obvious Mom had other things on her mind.

"I wanted to talk to you about Nathan," she said. "I've been thinking, and I have a suggestion to help you all get along better. And no, Tessa. It is *not* San Diego."

Tessa frowned.

Mom continued. "What I was thinking is that family relations are like international relations. For example, lately the United States has not been getting along with the government of a certain nearby nation. Now, what do you think my secretary of state has advised me to do?"

I thought of Nate. "Declare war?"

Mom gave me a look. "No, Cameron. What he suggests is that we *help* the other country—send experts and money to make their farms and roads and hospitals better."

"Nate hasn't got farms and roads and hospitals," Tessa said. "And I spent my allowance on pink boots. Remember?"

I helped Mom out. "Are you saying we should be nice to Nate?"

Mom nodded. "Exactly."

"I don't know much about other countries," Tessa said, "but I know my cousin, and that is a *dumb* idea."

"Tessa!" I said. "You can't say 'dumb' to the president."

"I didn't say 'dumb' to the president. I said 'dumb' to my mother. Aren't we supposed to express our opinions?"

"We're supposed to be polite," I said.

"Could I say something?" Mom asked.

"You should express your opinion," Tessa said.

Mom said thank you, she planned to, then, "I'm wondering if either of you has ever heard the saying,

'You catch more flies with honey than with vinegar'? It means nice often gets you what you want."

"So if we're nice, Nate will leave?" Tessa said.

Mom didn't say anything right away. I think she was counting to ten. Finally she took a breath. "Let's try an experiment," she said. "How about if you two are extra nice to Nate and we see what happens? One week only."

It's tough to say no when Mom is being reasonable. "One week only," I repeated. "Tessa?"

"One week only," Tessa grumbled.

All this time Mom had been sitting on Tessa's bed. Now Tessa twined both arms around mom's neck. Gently, Mom removed one arm, then the other. She gave Tessa a kiss. She came over and gave me one, too.

At the door, she said, "Good night, muffins," but I could tell already her mind had moved to other things—probably knocking heads together.

Our door closed.

Tessa whispered, "Cameron? I don't get it. Is Mom saying Nate's a fly?"

I yawned. "I think so. Sort of."

"That's what I thought," Tessa said. "So after we're done with being nice, we should try a different experiment."

"What's that?"

Tessa giggled. "A fly swatter."

CHAPTER NINE

THE next morning, Tessa started right in with nice. "Good morning, Cousin Nathan. May I get you a glass of orange juice?"

Nate is always the last one up. That day his eyes were barely open. He looked at Tessa through his lashes. "Are you sick or something?" he asked.

At the counter pouring milk, Granny said, "Nathan?"

"She's makin' fun of me!" he said.

Tessa's usual answer, *Am not,* would not have been nice. So instead, she pressed her lips together, got a glass from the cupboard, poured orange juice, set the glass at Nate's place and smiled a big sweet smile.

Granny had watched the whole performance. "What do you say, Nathan?" she asked.

Nate was suspicious, but with Granny watching, he had no choice. "Thanks," he mumbled.

Score one for nice!

When Tessa sat down, I reminded her we were going to start detecting after school. "You need to be thinking of questions," I said.

"Detecting what?" Nate asked.

I would have said, "None of your bee's wax," but I remembered nice. "Colonel Michaels's baton is missing," I said.

Nate's face turned serious all of a sudden. "His baton is missing?"

I looked at Tessa, and I knew it was killing her not to tell Nate how he'd been wrong about the baton.

It was killing me, too.

But telling him wouldn't exactly be nice—would it?

So instead I just said Colonel Michaels had asked us to investigate.

"Do you want to help us later?" Tessa asked, and my heart sank. I mean, there is such a thing as *too* nice.

But luckily, Nate said, "Uh . . . no. I'm kind of busy this afternoon."

And was I imagining it? Or did he have a weird look on his face?

At school, I had a fight with Courtney.

It started when I saw Kyle before the first bell, and he told me Courtney's dad had written about Hooligan on his blog.

We were standing around the flagpole. Tessa,

Nathan and I get there early so the Secret Service agents can get in position.

"The header says, 'Is First Dog Out of Control?'" Kyle said. "And then it says something like, 'Killer dog attacks unwary White House visitors and even steals their stuff!'"

Kyle's dad is a congressman, and Kyle's favorite books are biographies. He watches CNN and he reads *The Washington Post* at breakfast. No surprise he also reads Courtney's dad's blog.

"That's not true one bit!" I told him. "Hooligan just has too much energy."

"What did Hooligan steal?" Kyle asked.

"He didn't steal anything—he just grabbed markers," I was going to tell the whole story, but then I spotted Courtney. I am usually a wimp about fighting. But not if I have to defend my dog!

"Hey!" I waved. "I want to talk to you!"

Kyle is the kind of kid who stirs up trouble but doesn't stick around. He said, "I have to finish my homework," and left.

Courtney could see I was mad. She pointed at herself like, *Moi?*

I skipped explanations and got to the point. "Hooligan isn't vicious, and you know it, and it's not like you were bleeding or broke your arm or something."

Courtney seemed to know what I was talking about. "He knocked me down!" she said.

"Because you were too big of a klutz to get out of the way!"

"Klutz?!" Courtney said. "I'm the most graceful one in my tap class!"

"Who do you tap with? Elephants?"

After all that nice to Nate, I must've had meanness left over.

And besides, I was *mad*.

But Courtney gave it right back.

"You know what, Cameron? And I am only telling you this for your own good. Ever since your mom got elected president, you are so totally stuck up. You used to be a normal kid, but now you act like . . . I dunno, you're some kind of *princess*."

"That is *so not*—" I started to say, but Charlotte interrupted.

"Uh, Cameron? Courtney? Everything all right?"

Most of the time, the Secret Service agents stay out of the way. But there aren't a lot of teachers around before school.

I was embarrassed. "We're fine," I mumbled.

Courtney was not embarrassed. She pointed at Charlotte. "*See?* That proves it. You're such a princess someone has to protect you—even from your friends!"

Friends, I thought. Right.

Courtney and I stayed miles apart the rest of the day, and nothing especially horrible happened—except I had a lot to worry about.

Was Courtney right? Was I a princess?

And would Aunt Jen come through with Song Boys invitations?

And then there was Nate. How would I ever survive six more days of being nice?

After lunch, it was time to work on our bean sprout project. Evgenia was my partner, and our bean sprouts were growing nicely on their damp paper towel. While I measured them, she drew their picture.

"Ev," I said after a while. "Do you think I'm different since my mom got elected?"

Evgenia didn't look up. "Your mom?" she said. "Elected?"

I stared at her. Was it possible there was someone who didn't know . . . ?

But then she cracked up. "Just kidding," she said. "And no one could deny you're different, Cammie. *Wa-a-a-ay* different."

"Not that kind of different," I said. "Stuck-up different." I looked over at Courtney. "Do I act like I'm some kind of, like, *princess?*"

Evgenia saw me looking at Courtney. Then she looked back at her paper and drew a yellow circle outside the window. "The sun is what makes the sprouts grow," she explained.

"You're not answering my question," I said.

Evgenia stopped drawing. "You are better than some kids," she said. "Like at arithmetic and handwriting. And you're worse than anybody at spelling. You're pretty friendly, and you don't insult people on purpose." She shrugged. "But I never met a princess, so I don't know if that's what they're like."

I finished writing down sprout data. Evgenia drew the rays on her sun. Then she looked over at Courtney and back again. "I don't think you should worry about what some people say, Cammie. It isn't your fault your mom's the president. I mean, my parents didn't even vote for her."

CHAPTER TEN

AFTER school, I couldn't wait to start detecting.

But I had to.

It took Tessa forever to pick an outfit.

Our school doesn't make us wear uniforms. And usually when Tessa and I get home we don't bother to change. But Tessa loves clothes. For detecting, she claimed she needed something perfect.

"What do you think?" Standing in front of her closet, she struck a pose. She was wearing lime green cargo pants and a matching vest. Her T-shirt was black with a ladybug print, and her sneakers were yellow. "I thought a lot of pockets would be good," she added, "in case we have to collect evidence."

"Looks great," I said. "Can we go now? There's that dinner, and—"

"You don't sound sure," Tessa said. "What do detectives wear, anyway?"

"How should I know? Police uniforms probably."

Tessa turned back to her closet like maybe she'd find a police uniform.

"Would you *please* hurry up?" I said. "I know—Sherlock Holmes had a hat. Do you have a hat?"

Tessa grabbed a pink spangled baseball cap. "Like this?"

"Exactly," I said. "Let's go."

Tessa tugged the hat on. I grabbed my notebook.

"Who do we question first?" she asked.

"Mr. Bryant's on today. Let's take the elevator."

"But he wasn't in the East Room," Tessa said.

"It'll be like a warm-up."

If you're on the state or the ground floors, you have to have a key to call the presidential elevator. But on the upper floors, there are regular buttons.

"Good afternoon, young ladies," Mr. Bryant said when the doors opened. "You two are looking mighty serious this afternoon. Too much homework?"

"It's more important than homework, Mr. Bryant," said Tessa. "We are going to solve a mystery. And *you* are our first suspect."

"Mercy!" said Mr. Bryant.

"Not *suspect*, Tessa. *Witness*," I said.

"Oops." Tessa looked at Mr. Bryant again. "*You* are our first witness."

Mr. Bryant wiped pretend sweat from his forehead. "*Phew.*"

"Are you ready, Cammie?" Tessa asked.

"Ready."

Tessa crossed her arms over her chest. "Mr. Bryant,

where were you on the night of—what night was it, Cammie?"

"It wasn't night, it was afternoon. How about if we just explain what we're doing? Then after that we ask him what he knows."

Tessa explained, and Mr. Bryant shook his head. "Oh dear, oh dear—and that's not all that's disappeared. Mrs. Silver's all wrought up about the place cards for the mayors' dinner tonight. Hand-lettered, you know. They were bundled in a rubber band, she set them down, and . . ."—he snapped his fingers—"like that, they were gone!"

I didn't think missing place cards were too tragic, but I said, "That's too bad."

And Tessa asked, "Where were they before they disappeared?"

"I believe it was the State Dining Room," Mr. Bryant said.

"Colonel Michaels's baton disappeared from the East Room on Tuesday," Tessa told Mr. Bryant. "So have you seen any baton thieves since Tuesday, Mr. Bryant? Stupid baton thieves, I mean, because Granny told us most criminals are stupid."

Mr. Bryant rubbed his cheek. "I can't say that I have," he said. "Not that I'd exactly know what a stupid baton thief looks like . . . unless the thief were to be *carrying* the baton. Now, that would be a definite clue. Or—what about this?—a person carrying something in which a baton might be hidden."

I was writing all this down.

"Something long and skinny," Tessa said.

Mr. Bryant nodded. "You might also be looking," he went on, "in the places where a thief could hide something long and skinny."

The elevator had been going up and down for a while. Now it arrived back at the state floor. Mr. Bryant opened the doors. Tessa was saying thanks when I spotted something yellow on the floor and picked it up.

"What've you got there?" Mr. Bryant squinted.

"Looks like flower petals," I said. "Kind of mangled."

"Our first clue!" Tessa said. "I'll put them in a pocket."

I handed them over.

"Thanks again, Mr. Bryant," I said.

"You're quite welcome. And at the first sign of a stupid baton thief, I'll know where to report."

CHAPTER ELEVEN

STEPPING out of the elevator, we saw we were in luck. In the foyer was the White House's big old grand piano, and one of our witnesses, Mrs. Hedges, was dusting it.

"Go ahead and ask your questions," Mrs. Hedges said after Tessa explained. "Only I'll keep working if you don't mind. They'll be moving the piano to the East Room for the concert, and it has to look good."

Tessa crossed her arms over her chest. "Mrs. Hedges," she said, "did *you* see anyone suspicious sneaking off with Colonel Michaels's baton on Tuesday? Or anyone suspicious sneaking off with something long and skinny where Colonel Michaels's baton could hide?"

Mrs. Hedges wasn't listening. She had set down the duster and was looking around for something. "Well, *that's* a puzzle," she said. "The polish is right here." She pointed at a round can on the piano bench.

"And I could have sworn the cloth was with it. Where did it go?"

"We'll help you look," Tessa said. And we did—we even opened up the bench.

No cloth. But underneath the piano, I found another pile of petals.

"This one used to be a daffodil," I said.

Tessa took it and looked up at me. "I'm getting a bad feeling," she said.

Have I mentioned Hooligan loves flowers?

Mrs. Hedges sat down on the piano bench. "Go ahead with your questions, girls. Then I'll get a new cloth from supplies."

Tessa asked again about anyone suspicious. This time Mrs. Hedges listened, but she didn't answer. Instead, she said, "I don't think you're doing this right."

In my family, Mom and I are the patient ones. Tessa is more like Aunt Jen and Granny. Now she was getting exasperated. "We're doing exactly what Granny told us!"

"That's as may be," said Mrs. Hedges. "But what you *ought* to ask me is if I've seen anything strange since Tuesday. I read a lot of mystery books, so I know."

"*Fine,*" Tessa said. "Have you seen anything strange since Tuesday?"

Mrs. Hedges thought for a minute. "Well, it's strange that my polishing cloth is missing. Don't you think?"

When Mrs. Hedges had gone, Tessa went drama. "*She was no help!*"

"We don't know for sure till we look at the notes," I said, "but it's true, asking questions is harder than I thought. Let's see who's in the dining room."

There are two dining rooms on the state floor of the White House: the State Dining Room, which is on the west side, and a smaller one next to it. That was where we found Mr. Patel and Mr. Kane setting up for the night's dinner.

"*Buona sera, bambine,*" said Mr. Kane. "That means, 'Good evening, children.' Your mom has invited some very important mayors to eat with her a very Italian supper."

Mr. Kane is medium old with a round face and floppy hair. Mr. Patel is kind of young and really handsome. Aunt Jen says he has a million-megawatt smile. Now he was setting out baskets of breadsticks on tables laid with checkered tablecloths.

I thought of what Mr. Bryant had said—a place to hide something long and skinny. How about a basket of breadsticks?

"Where did the breadsticks come from?" I asked Mr. Kane.

"Made them myself this morning," he said.

So much for that idea. The baton went missing Tuesday.

"Would you care for a sample?" Mr. Kane asked us.

Tessa and I were feeling cookie-deprived. "Yes!" we answered at the same time.

The breadsticks were delicious. Done chewing, I opened my notebook and waited for Tessa to explain about detecting—only she didn't. When I looked over, she was grinning stupidly at Mr. Patel.

Oh, brother. Tessa is only seven. Normal kids don't get crushes till they're nine at least.

"Tessa!" I hissed.

"What? Oh! Sorry—Mr. Patel, have you ever seen any stupid batons running around suspiciously lately?"

"Excuse me?" asked Mr. Patel.

I rolled my eyes. Tessa's brain was clearly scrambled. I would have to do the talking.

"Did I see anything strange on Tuesday?" Mr. Patel repeated my question. "Only your X-treme dog."

"Same goes for me," said Mr. Kane. "And as for stolen, all that's missing around here are cookies from a tray."

I looked up from writing. "Really?"

Mr. Kane shrugged. "But I don't see what that has to do with Colonel Michaels's baton."

"I don't either," I said. "It's only that a lot of stuff is missing lately."

Mr. Kane looked at his watch. "The mayors are due at six, girls. Do you have more questions?"

"That's all for now," I said. "Thank you."

"And we really really really appreciate it." Tessa was back to staring at Mr. Patel.

"Yeah—*really.*" I tugged her arm. "Let's see if we can find Mr. Baney or Mr. Ross."

CHAPTER TWELVE

THE flower shop is on the ground floor. The fastest way to get there is through the cross hall and down the main stairs. We were on our way down when we saw them—yellow petals everywhere, a daffodil disaster!

"I told you I had a bad feeling," said Tessa.

And sure enough, here came Mr. Baney carrying a huge bouquet. Only it wasn't a bouquet of flowers. It was a bouquet of stems.

"That dog of yours!" he thundered.

Mr. Baney is six feet four inches tall and played football in college. He already doesn't like Hooligan on account of something that happened last month with a vase, some roses and a cabinet secretary.

"Have you seen him?" I asked.

"No, I haven't," said Mr. Baney, "and he'll stay out of sight if he knows what's good for him." He waved the stems. "Look at what's left of my beautiful arrangement!"

"We can help clean up," Tessa said.

Mr. Baney likes Tessa. He thinks she has "flair." He calmed down a little.

"I appreciate the offer, but the staff will do it. Meanwhile, I just ran into Mrs. Hedges. She said you girls are detecting. Something about a missing baton?"

"That's right," said Tessa, and then she explained.

Mr. Baney shook his head. "I'm afraid I didn't notice anything out of the ordinary," he said. "Are you quite sure your dog didn't take it?"

"We were holding him when it disappeared," I said.

Mr. Baney shrugged. "I wish I could be more helpful."

My watch said 5:30. There were still a few minutes before the mayors would be arriving. We went back up the stairs to look for Mr. Ross. His office is by the North Portico, but he wasn't there. Leaving it, we ran into Nate. He was coming from the Blue Room and heading for the stairs.

"What are you doing down here?" I asked. "I thought you were busy after school."

Nate didn't look at us. He just kept walking. "Uh . . . I am busy," he mumbled, "and now I'm going upstairs . . . to be more busy."

When he was gone, Tessa looked at me. "Our cousin has issues."

I was going to agree, but I never had the chance. Two men wearing gray suits came into the cross hall from the East Room. I had never seen them before, which was unusual. Even though more than a hundred people work in the White House, most of them look familiar.

I was about to ask Tessa if she knew them when Randy, another Secret Service agent, appeared. "Please," he said to the men, "could you follow me? I think there has been some confusion."

The men didn't seem to understand at first—didn't they speak English?—but finally they followed him out.

"Could they be our stupid baton thieves?" Tessa asked.

"I don't know," I said. "I'm like Mr. Bryant—not sure what stupid baton thieves look like."

CHAPTER THIRTEEN

IN our family, we never eat dinner till 6:30 or 7. Granny believes we will wake up hungry in the night if we eat earlier. So when Tessa and I got back upstairs, we had time to apply logic. The striped sofa in the West Sitting Hall seemed like a good place for this. It is soft and cozy, good for thinking.

Hooligan was in the West Sitting Hall, too, sound asleep in his bed. To look at him, you'd never believe the damage he does to daffodils.

"Do you think he stole the other stuff, too, Cammie?" Tessa asked. "The place cards and the polishing cloth?"

"Don't forget the cookies," I said. "And no, I don't. Most times when Hooligan steals something, we find it right away—like the flowers."

"I don't think we're ever gonna find those cookies," Tessa said.

"Good point," I said. "And we know he didn't steal the baton."

"Do you think there's more than one thief in the White House?" Tessa asked.

"That doesn't seem logical," I said. "Let's look at our notes."

It's not easy to write fast standing up. So even though I have good handwriting (ask Evgenia), my notes were kind of a mess. After I crossed out the unimportant stuff, this is what was left:

1) *Mr. Bryant's eyesight is not very good.*
2) *No witnesses had seen anything strange Tuesday afternoon. (Mostly they were too busy chasing Hooligan.)*
3) *It's not only the baton that's missing. Also: place cards, polishing cloth, cookies.*
4) *Mrs. Hedges is exasperating.*
5) *Mayors like Italian food.*
6) *A basket of breadsticks would be a good place to hide something long and skinny.*
7) *Tessa has a crush on Mr. Patel.*
8) *Hooligan wrecked the daffodils and scattered petals everywhere.*
9) *Hooligan makes Mr. Baney grumpy.*
10) *Nate was on the state floor this afternoon. (Why?)*
11) *And so were two men wearing gray suits.*

Tessa made me cross out the part about Mr. Patel. Then we stared at the list for a while.

Finally I said, "Logic isn't helping."

"I know," Tessa said. "Maybe we need more witnesses."

"There's Mr. Ross," I said.

"And what about Nate?" Tessa said.

"You're right—he was in the East Room Tuesday. Only he wasn't there the whole time, remember? When we were holding Hooligan, he kind of disappeared."

Tessa said, "Yeah, that was strange." Then she looked up. "Hey, we've been asking people about 'strange' all afternoon, and there it is!"

I was going to say Nate would never steal anything. But then I thought of something logical. "Tessa—remember how you thought they'd have to cancel The Song Boys? I mean because the baton was missing."

"When I still thought it was the Who-za baton," Tessa said.

"Sousa. Right. It was Nate who told us that the Band can't play without it."

Tessa nodded. "But now we know that isn't true."

"*We* know that," I said. "But Nate doesn't. He wasn't there when we talked to Colonel Michaels. And after that, we never told him. I bet he still thinks if the baton is gone, then The Song Boys can't play."

Tessa's eyes got big. "And besides that—remember?—he told us he hoped something would happen so they *can't* play!"

For a moment, the only sound was Hooligan woofing in his sleep. Finally, Tessa said what we were both thinking: "What if Nate took the baton so they'd have to cancel The Song Boys?"

I didn't answer right away. I might hate my cousin. But I couldn't believe he would steal anything.

Tessa, on the other hand, could totally believe it.

"There's only one question left," she said, "what did he do with the baton?"

I wanted my sister to slow down, but she was on a roll.

"When he came out of the Blue Room today, he wouldn't say what he was doing," Tessa went on. "You know what I think? The baton is in the Blue Room!"

"Tessa, that's nuts."

"It's not! Look, Cammie, here's what happened. When Hooligan did the frenzy on Tuesday, Nate grabbed the baton. Then he had to hide it fast. He couldn't carry it upstairs because anybody might see him. So he hid it someplace downstairs."

"Oka-a-ay," I said. "But what does that have to do with him being down there today?"

"Maybe he was making sure it was still there—that we hadn't found it," Tessa said. "He wasn't carrying anything when we saw him. So it's *still* down there. Come on!" Tessa jumped to her feet, but at the same time, Granny came in and said we should go wash up.

"Granny," Tessa announced, "there is an emergency. I am afraid we will have to delay dinner."

Granny was not impressed. "And what is this so-called emergency?"

"Nate stole Colonel Michaels's baton and hid it," Tessa said. "And now Cammie and I must go and get it back."

CHAPTER FOURTEEN

GRANNY'S answer was dead silence.

Not a good sign.

Finally, Tessa said, "Are you angry at Nate?"

"No," Granny said.

"Are you angry at us?"

"Yes," Granny said.

And then she let us have it. "You girls have been out to get that boy since we moved into the White House. His behavior hasn't been perfect, goodness knows. But I can hardly blame him if he feels ganged up on."

Unlike me, Tessa is not a wimp. If someone gets mad at her, she gets mad back. "In my opinion"—she put her hands on her hips—"Nate stole that baton."

"And in *my* opinion . . ." Granny's hands were on her hips, too. "*You* are full of prunes, Tessa Parks! Your cousin—my grandson—is not a thief. And that is the last I want to hear on the subject. Understood?" She looked at Tessa first, then me.

We looked at our shoes. "Understood," we said meekly.

And we also understood that there would be no more detecting that night.

Dinner was not so fun. Granny didn't once crack a smile, and Tessa and I were half afraid to talk. Besides the fancy Italian noodles, the only good thing was that Nate didn't eat with us. According to Granny, he was having some kind of an extra piano lesson.

An extra piano lesson?

Here in America in the twenty-first century, I am one of two kids my age who does not have a phone.

Nate is the other.

Supposedly, we are too young. And all the excellent arguments about why we need them (like being the only person without one is ruining my social life!!!) do not convince our parents.

Nate and Aunt Jen have their own family phone upstairs. People call me on our family's phone. Usually when it rings for me, it's Courtney. But that night it wasn't.

"Cameron? This is Colonel Michaels. How are you?"

I was sitting on the floor doing homework. Picturing Colonel Michaels, I sat up straight. "Fine, sir, how are you?"

"Very well, thank you. I was just wondering whether you've had any success with the baton."

Tessa was sitting beside me. Granny was in a chair across the room. There was a book in her lap, but I knew she was listening. If I mentioned Nate, she'd go ballistic.

"Not exactly success," I said. "But today we interviewed witnesses and applied logic."

"Ah," said Colonel Michaels.

"And, tomorrow, uh . . ." I looked at Tessa for help, but she shrugged and shook her head. "Well, tomorrow . . . our plan is to find it once and for all."

"Splendid," said Colonel Michaels. "Then perhaps you could meet me just prior to the concert? And bring the baton with you."

What I said was, "No problem," but what I thought was, *I hope*.

Mom still hadn't come upstairs when we went to bed, so once again, Granny said good night. She had barely closed the door when Tessa rolled over. "It's in the Blue Room!"

I wasn't so sure. But I didn't have a better idea. "The three color rooms connect," I reminded her. "Nate could have been in Red or Green for all we know."

"You're right," said Tessa. "How about this? Pretend you're Nate on the state floor on Tuesday. You need a good hiding place in a hurry. Where do you go?"

I didn't have to think, I just knew. It was something Granny had shown me, Nate and Tessa the first week we moved in. Even then, I had thought what a brilliant place it would be to hide something.

"The worktable," I said.

I couldn't see my sister in the dark, but I could feel her smiling. "Cammie—you're a genius!"

CHAPTER FIFTEEN

GRANNY doesn't usually stay mad for long, and she was in a better mood at breakfast—especially after she saw us acting super nice to Nate.

Weirdly, Nate was pretty nice himself. Like in the van on the way to school, Granny gave me my last spelling quiz before the test—and he didn't show off and spell words before I could.

Did he maybe feel guilty about stealing the baton?

Then at school, something good happened. *Finally!*

On everybody's desk except mine and Nate's were thick, cream-colored envelopes with the return address, "The White House," in blue. Courtney had one. And so did Ms. Nicols.

Inside were fancy printed invitations:

*President Marilee Parks, Mr. Richard Parks
and Ms. Jennifer Leone
Request the pleasure of your presence at
a performance by The Song Boys
In support of literacy
2 P.M. on Saturday
The East Room of the White House
1600 Pennsylvania Avenue
Refreshments to follow*

Score, Aunt Jen!

Right away the girls started talking about what they were going to wear. And the boys started talking about what they were going to eat.

For a little while, I got to be the hero! And Nate didn't even spoil it by calling The Song Boys bubblegum.

But at recess, Courtney said, "When they're done singing, do we get face time?"

And Alexander said, "If there's pizza, I can't have tomatoes. I'm allergic."

And after recess, Ms. Nicols said, "I'm sure everyone would really appreciate it if The Song Boys would take a few minutes to answer questions. Can that be arranged, Cameron?"

So much for being a hero. I told them all the same thing: "I don't know. It's up to Aunt Jen and Mrs. Silver."

The spelling test was after lunch. I thought after Granny had quizzed me so much, I would ace it. But

I couldn't concentrate. And no matter how I arranged the letters, the words kept looking wrong.

"How did it go?" Granny asked in the van later.

"I don't want to talk about it," I said.

♫

Tessa and I wanted to go detecting as soon as we got home. But what were we going to tell Granny? And how would we get rid of Nate?

Luckily, Nate disappeared upstairs right after our snack. And when we asked for permission to go downstairs, Granny said okay. She knew Colonel Michaels had called. And we were careful not to remind her about our number one suspect.

This time Tessa didn't bother to change clothes. She just grabbed her pink Sherlock Holmes hat, and we raced downstairs to the Green Room.

In case you're wondering, I am not normally a person who thinks furniture is interesting. You sit on it, eat on it, put a book on it. Besides that, who cares?

But the worktable in the Green Room is different. I noticed it when Granny explained it was the same design as her grandmother's sewing box—but bigger.

Tessa had asked, "Did your grandmother know she had a rare and historic antique?"

And Granny pointed out, "She thought it was the latest high-tech gadget."

Now, Tessa and I were beside the table.

"Ready?" Tessa asked.

"Be careful," I said. "It's historic."

"*Duh,*" Tessa said, "like what isn't around here?"

Carefully, she removed the lamp on top and set it on the floor. Next, she lifted the tabletop, then together we unfolded all the bits and pieces to reveal . . . about a million hidden compartments! That's what makes this the superhero of furniture: mild-mannered table on the outside, secret transformer on the inside.

I wasn't disappointed when we didn't find the baton right away. Nate would have hidden it better than that. But after we one-by-one opened every lid and drawer, I had to admit I was wrong.

"Guess I'm not such a genius," I said. "But maybe the bad guy isn't Nate? Granny says criminals are stupid, and Nate isn't."

"But I don't know anybody stupid!" Tessa whined.

"Mom says Hooligan's not too bright," I said.

Tessa looked around. "*Shhh!* You'll hurt his feelings! And anyway, I meant a person."

I shrugged. "Mostly, the White House is full of smart people—unless you believe what Courtney's dad writes in his blog."

"Maybe Courtney's dad took the baton? Or what about Courtney?"

"Why would they do that?" I said. "And besides, the baton disappeared on Tuesday. Courtney hasn't even been here since Monday."

Tessa tapped her head. "Way to apply logic, Cammie. I know—those men in the gray suits. Who were they, anyway?"

"They weren't carrying any baton," I said. "They weren't carrying anything."

"That means if they did steal it—they had to have hidden it," Tessa said. "I know—what about the fireplaces?"

This was a smart idea. Almost every room on the state floor has one—and they're all full of kindling. Kindling would make excellent camouflage for a baton.

We started with the Green Room then fanned out.

Poking around fireplaces is dusty. It hurts your knees. Plus I got a splinter. I had just finished up in the Red Room when I heard Tessa squeal.

Did she find it?

"Where are you?"

"East Room! Hurry!"

CHAPTER SIXTEEN

THERE are many famous paintings in the East Room, including one of the Martha Washington looking serious. When I ran in, she was looking serious at Tessa.

"What is it? What did you find?"

"There." Tessa pointed.

I had to stare before I saw them: two plastic legs with gold zip-up boots. They were frozen in a scissor kick, sticking straight up from the kindling.

"Astronaut Barbie," said Tessa. "Can you get her? I'm afraid to look."

"Shut your eyes," I said and pulled Barbie from the rubble.

Tessa peeked through her lashes. "Is it bad?"

"She'll live," I said. "It's good she was wearing a helmet."

"Let me see," Tessa said, and I handed her over. Barbie was in one piece, but her spacesuit was a mess. Tessa licked her thumb and wiped a smudge off. "Could she be a clue?"

"A clue that Hooligan grabs stuff and drops it," I said. "But we already know that."

By now we had looked in every fireplace, and it was getting late. We decided to do one more walk through of the state floor before we went upstairs. In the Blue Room, we found Mr. Ross—the one witness we hadn't interviewed! He was looking back and forth between two vases on a mantle.

"Hello, girls," he said. "Do these look lined up wrong to you?"

I thought they were fine, but Tessa said, "The left one's too far forward."

Mr. Ross reached up and made the adjustment. "Thank you." Then he spotted Tessa's beat-up Barbie. "Hooligan?"

Tessa nodded. "We found her in a fireplace."

"I trust she'll make a full recovery," said Mr. Ross. "In the meantime, I understand you girls were looking for me."

Tessa explained that we were investigating. Then she crossed her arms over her chest. "Mr. Ross, did you notice anything strange on Tuesday afternoon?"

"Only that Hooligan came out of nowhere!" Mr. Ross shook his head. "It's a good thing we know that dog's on our side. I've mentioned the missing items to the Secret Service, and they've been talking security breach."

"Security what?" Tessa asked.

"Now there's no need to worry," said Mr. Ross. "But let's say we really had a thief in the White House. We'd have to restrict access till the problem was resolved."

This time Tessa looked at me. "'Access'?"

"People coming to visit," I said.

Tessa waved her hands the way she does. *"Like for example The Song Boys?"*

"Now, girls, I'm sorry. I didn't mean to upset you," said Mr. Ross. "It's just that Mrs. Silver was beside herself over those place cards. And then there's the baton. . . . But the other items are trivial, and I'm sure there's no cause for alarm. Do you have more questions?"

We didn't. So Mr. Ross wished us good luck and headed for his office. We were right behind him till Tessa stopped and looked back over her shoulder.

"Cammie," she said, "who would move one of those vases, anyway?"

"I dunno," I said. "Somebody dusting?"

Tessa shook her head. "The maids are super careful. And Granny said a clue could be something out of place. Those vases are tall and they have lids. Wouldn't a baton just fit?"

One second later, I was reaching for a vase. When I lifted the lid, I saw there *was* something inside: a poor, dead, dried-out fly.

Because she takes ballet, Tessa is good at standing on her tiptoes. But she is shorter than me and bobbled her vase. If it broke, Aunt Jen would kill us . . . but finally Tessa got a grip. Then she lifted the lid, looked inside, and said, "I see something, Cammie!"

"The baton?"

Tessa reached in and . . . it was not the baton. It

was something shorter and fatter that was wrapped in a napkin. Carefully, Tessa unfolded the napkin and revealed . . .

. . . six cookies?

Score, Cammie and Tessa!

But wait—were they green and stale?

Tessa inspected them one by one. Then, bravely, she tried a nibble. After she swallowed, I counted to ten. When she didn't double over or throw up, I took one and tried it, too.

Delicious!

It took approximately thirty seconds for us to devour all six cookies. I was wiping the last crumbs from my lips when I thought of something. "Wait a sec, Tess. If those are the missing cookies from yesterday—"

"—then we just ate the evidence!" Tessa said.

But the cookies didn't have anything to do with the baton.

Did they?

Before I could ponder that question, I had something new to think about—a loud buzz from outside that finally changed into *WOP-wop WOP-wop WOP-wop*.

Helicopters! And they were coming this way!

"We'd better hurry," I said to Tessa, and we ran for the stairs.

CHAPTER SEVENTEEN

HELICOPTERS can only mean one thing on Friday afternoon.

Daddy's home!

The helicopter that carries the president is called Marine One. A helicopter carrying anybody else in our family is called Marine One Foxtrot. *F* for *foxtrot*, *F* for *family*. Get it?

No matter who's inside, the helicopters travel in a group, and nobody knows which one has passengers. This is supposed to fool bad guys.

It also fools Tessa and me. Usually when we try to guess which one Mom or Dad is in, we are wrong.

Granny and Malik—he's another Secret Service agent—were at the Dip Room door when we got there.

"The one on the left?" Malik guessed.

"I think the one in the middle," I said.

"I vote with Cammie," Tessa said.

The helicopter rotors slowed, and their whirlwind

died. Finally, the hatches opened—and Dad emerged from the one on the left.

"*Yesss!*" Malik said.

"How do you *do* that?" Tessa asked.

Malik grinned. "The Secret Service has its secrets."

Dad waved to the news guys, came down the steps, stopped and looked toward the Rose Garden. My mom's office—the Oval Office—is on the other side of it and, right on schedule, Mom was walking out the door. When she reached Dad, she gave him a squeeze and a kiss, then the two of them walked toward us holding hands while cameras flashed and whirred.

It's pretty much the same every Friday.

"*Daddy!*" Tessa and I grabbed him around the waist. He kissed Granny's cheek. More cameras flashed. Then he let go, looked around and asked, "Where's your cousin?"

Tessa said, "Who cares?"

Granny gave Tessa a warning look.

Tessa whined to Mom. "It's not fair I have to be nice if he's not even here!"

"Nathan is practicing piano," Granny told Dad.

Dad looked from Granny to Tessa to Mom and asked, "So what did I miss this week?"

The president of the United States is a very busy person. She has to travel, give speeches, be on TV and have meetings. She has to read reports. And she has to boss people around.

Granny and Aunt Jen agree that Mom has always been good at that last part.

You might already have figured out that because Mom is busy, Tessa and I don't see her as much as we want to.

And sometimes we miss her.

But Friday is family night. And if she possibly can, Mom stays in with Tessa and Dad and me. We play Monopoly and talk about soccer and ballet and congress, just like any other family. The only difference is the pizza comes from the White House kitchen.

I love Fridays. For one thing, I rule at Monopoly.

But this Friday was different.

I had too much to think about!

Where was Colonel Michaels's baton?

How did the cookies get in the vase?

Was there really a thief in the White House?

My brain was so busy, I forgot to collect rent on my hotels. And Tessa was just as bad. She was banker, and didn't pay up when we passed GO.

The third time she forgot, Dad said, "What's on your mind, Tess?"

My sister didn't hesitate. "Is it true The Song Boys can't play if there's a thief in the White House?"

Dad looked at Mom. "Do you know what she's talking about?"

Mom looked at Tessa. "Remind me. Who are The Song Boys?"

"*Mo-o-o-om!*" Tessa and I said at the same time.

"I'm sorry," she said. "Is that the literacy event? I have a full calendar tomorrow."

Taking turns, we reminded her about the concert. Then we told her about the missing stuff and what Mr. Ross had said.

"Ah," Mom said when we were done. "Now I see. And I admit it's mysterious. But none of it rises to the level of security breach. I think your concert will happen right on . . . ." The last word dissolved in a yawn. "I'm sorry, muffins. I'm tired, and I have a meeting at the crack of dawn. The president of a certain nearby nation is coming for a White House tour. And my advisers tell me I should handle it personally."

"Must be a big shot," Dad said.

"Sort of," Mom said. "Do you girls remember what I told you the other night?"

"The country we're not getting along with?" I said.

"Exactly," Mom said.

"Let me get this straight," Tessa said. "We're sending money for farms, roads and hospitals, plus you have to give a personal White House tour? Not getting along with the United States is a good deal!"

"Not getting along with us is a good deal for Nate, too," I said. "We have to be super nice. He doesn't have to do a thing."

"It's only for a week," Mom said.

"Five days, one hour and . . ." I looked at my watch. ". . . eighteen minutes to go."

It was two turns later that I went bankrupt. Two turns after that, Tessa did, too. In our family losers put the game away, so—after Mom gave us kisses and went to bed—Tessa and I rubber banded money piles. Meanwhile, Dad was getting Hooligan ready for his walk.

"Girls?" Dad was kneeling by Hooligan's bed. He did not sound happy.

Tessa and I knew what was coming.

"Yes, Daddykins?" Tessa said.

"We love you, Daddy," I said.

"Hmmph," Dad said. "If you love me—and if you love Hooligan—you can show it by cleaning out his bed." He waved his hand in front of his nose. "*Phew!*"

I said, "It's Tessa's turn!" and she said, "I did it last time!" and I said, "That was the *other* last—"

Dad held up his hand. "I have an idea. How about if the two of you do your chore *together?*"

Tessa yawned dramatically. "I'm *so-o-o-o* sleepy!"

Dad said, "Tomorrow after soccer and ballet."

"And lunch," I said.

"And Song Boys," Tessa said.

"Before dinner tomorrow!" Dad said. "Promise?"

We promised.

Then Dad and Hooligan left for the South Lawn.

A few minutes later, Tessa and I were putting on jammies when I heard the family phone ring. By then,

Dad was back. I heard him talking, then a knock. Our door opened.

"It's Courtney," Dad said. "She claims it's an emergency."

An emergency apology? Today at school we didn't even talk to each other. I reached, but Dad handed the phone to Tessa.

Huh?

Tessa didn't say anything at first, just listened. Finally, she shook her head. "Well *duh* they're designer, but jeans still aren't appropriate."

Oh—so that was it. She didn't want to apologize at all. She wanted fashion advice.

"I can't help it if that's the same thing your mom said." Tessa listened some more then shrugged. "Okay, sorry." Now, she handed the phone to me.

"I hate all my dresses!" Courtney whined. "If I have to wear one, I'm not coming."

Did I mention Courtney can be as dramatic as Tessa? And just as annoying.

"*And* you're sorry we had that fight yesterday?" I said.

There was a pause. I bet she was trying to remember the fight. "Oh yeah," she finally said. "You're not really that much of a princess."

Now I had a choice. I could decide that was a good enough apology, or I could keep fighting. I was too tired to keep fighting. "I forgive you," I said. *For now,* I thought.

CHAPTER EIGHTEEN

TESSA woke me the next morning.

"I bet Colonel Michaels hasn't told the rest of the band the baton is even missing," she said.

"I am still sleeping," I said.

"Well, okay," Tessa said, "but I am still talking."

I opened my eyes and looked at my sister. "Why wouldn't Colonel Michaels tell the band?"

"He's embarrassed that he lost it," Tessa said. "You know—like that time when my ballet shoe was gone and the recital was coming up? I didn't tell anybody."

"I don't think grown-ups are like that," I said.

"Why not?" she said. "Grown-ups are bigger than kids. But they're still people."

"I forget what happened with your ballet shoe that time."

"I was too embarrassed to tell Granny till we were leaving," Tessa said. "We found it in the end, but we were late, and my teacher was so mad!"

I was going to ask where she finally found the shoe,

but the alarm beeped. I hit the button. "I've got one idea left," I said. "It probably won't work. Plus it will get us in trouble."

"I've got an idea, too," Tessa said. "Give up."

"We promised Colonel Michaels!"

"I know." Tessa sighed. "What's your idea?"

"We ask Nate right out if he took the baton. And then we hope he confesses."

Tessa nodded. "It will never work, and it will get us in trouble for not being nice. But . . ." She paused dramatically. ". . . it's our only hope!"

While I brushed my teeth and put on my soccer uniform, I tried to think of the best way to ask my *so superior* cousin if he was a thief. Getting the words right would be tricky. I had to surprise him into confessing but not surprise him into socking me.

I practiced in front of the mirror a couple of times. Then I headed for breakfast.

Tessa was already at the table. When I sat down, I saw no place was set for Nate.

"Isn't Nate eating with us?" I asked.

Dad was at the head of the table, hidden behind *The Washington Post*. "He's got some special project or other. He's supposed to be back after lunch."

Tessa looked at me. "Now can we give up?"

I said no, but I was just being stubborn. Truthfully? I was out of ideas.

As usual, Granny went to ballet with Tessa, and Dad came to soccer with me. Like always, Secret Service agents have to come with both of us. That day, Dad and Malik cheered like crazy, but my team, the D.C. Destroyers got D.C. Destroyed—4–1.

Meanwhile, at ballet, Tessa took a wrong leap and knocked over the girl next to her.

Back home Tessa and I took showers. We dried our hair. We ate lunch. Then it was time to get dressed for The Song Boys.

I should have been so excited!

Instead, I was so miserable. Tessa and I had bragged to Colonel Michaels about our detecting skills. We had promised we would find his baton. How could we tell him we had failed?

If your mom is the president, you can't always choose what you wear. For "public occasions"—the ones with photographers and lots of people—Aunt Jen picks for us. Our clothes for The Song Boys concert were laid out on the bed. For Tessa, there was a pink skirt and a pink sweater and tights with pink flowers. She saw her outfit and squealed. Tessa loves pink.

For me, there was a boring blue dress with pockets, white tights with blue flowers and a boring white sweater.

I did not squeal. And when I tugged on the dress, it was itchy.

"Hurry up," I said to Tessa. She was fixing her hair. "If we go now, there's time to look for Nate."

Tessa put her brush down. "If we take the elevator, we can say hi to Mr. Bryant."

Hooligan was waiting outside our bedroom and followed us. It was Tessa's turn to press the elevator button, but before she could, something amazing happened—something unbelievable: Hooligan sat back on his haunches, leaned forward so his front paws hit the wall, and then, with the tip of his wet black nose, he pressed the button himself!

CHAPTER NINETEEN

TESSA and I were still staring when the elevator door opened.

"Hello, young ladies. Hello, Hooligan," Mr. Bryant greeted us. "How are all of you this fine afternoon?"

Hooligan trotted through the door. Mr. Bryant grinned and gave him a dog biscuit from his pocket.

Tessa and I spoke at once: "*Mr. Bryant, Hooligan just—*"

"*Mr. Bryant, did you know Hooligan can—*"

"Call the elevator?" Mr. Bryant chuckled. "You're no dummy, are you, Hooligan? You know I've got biscuits."

Hooligan wagged his tail, and Mr. Bryant gave him another one. "Your pup gives as good as he gets, though—brings me treats, too. Napkins mostly. The occasional Barbie. Sticks sometimes."

"He brings you treats? What do you do with 'em?" I asked.

Mr. Bryant counted on his fingers. "Cloth napkins

I return to the laundry," he said. "Barbies I give to one of the maids. Sticks and miscellaneous? Hooligan gets to keep those."

"Does Hooligan use the elevator a lot?" I asked.

Mr. Bryant shrugged. "I like to have the company."

"Cammie, do you get it?" Tessa asked. "*This* is where Hooligan goes when he's AWOL!"

"One mystery solved," I said.

The door opened. "State floor," said Mr. Bryant.

Tessa said, "Coming, Hooligan?" But Hooligan had curled up all cozy in the corner.

"Suit yourself," I told him. "Bye, Mr. Bryant!"

"Good-bye, young ladies. And I do hope the music's not *too* loud."

The cross hall was empty except for Charlotte standing at the East Room doors. They were closed.

Tessa and I ran up to her. "You'll never guess!" Tessa said. "When Hooligan goes AWOL, he's in the elevator with Mr. Bryant!"

Charlotte laughed. "No lie?"

Tessa crossed her pinkie fingers in front of her face. "No lie!"

I looked at the doors. "Are *they* in there?" I whispered.

Charlotte shook her head. "Their flight was delayed, but they're on their way. And the Marine Band musicians are setting up."

I took a deep breath for courage. "We need to talk to Colonel Michaels."

Charlotte opened the door a crack and winked.

"Okay, but—" She cocked her head, listening to something on her earpiece. Then her face got serious.

"What is it?" Tessa asked.

"Nothing to worry about," she said, but she closed the door. "I think for now you'd better stay out here."

Tessa was going to argue, but she got distracted. "Cammie, look!"

From out of the Blue Room came Nate. He was frowning. There was a napkin in his hand. He was wearing a tie and jacket and khakis.

At last! My big chance to confront him!

But I froze. What was that speech I practiced?

Luckily, Tessa hadn't practiced at all. Now she crossed her arms over her chest and faced him. "Cousin Nathan," she said. "Did *you* steal Colonel Michaels's baton?"

Like I expected, he was surprised.

But not half as surprised as me about one second later. "Yes, I did," he said. "And now they'll have to cancel The Song Boys. And it's all my fault. And I feel awful."

Tessa looked at me. "Your terrible plan worked, Cammie!"

I wanted to tell Nate, *You should feel awful!* but there was no time for that. "Where is it?" I demanded.

For a long second, Nate didn't answer. Finally, he looked at his toes. "Gone."

CHAPTER TWENTY

TESSA and I would have pounded Nate—except for one thing.

The Secret Service is well trained.

"Settle down, girls," Charlotte said after she had hold of us. "Let's see what he's got to say. Go ahead, Nate."

"I took it when everybody was cleaning up after Hooligan on Tuesday," he said. "Colonel Michaels had set it down, and no one was looking. I wanted to keep The Song Boys from playing because I hated their music, plus I was mad at you guys—"

"Yeah, yeah, we know all that," said Tessa. "*Where is it?*"

"That's what I'm trying to tell you!" Nate said. "I don't know! I hid it in one of the big East Room fireplaces. But I changed my mind, and Thursday I went back to get it—only it was gone."

"The fireplace?" Tessa said. "That's where we found Astronaut Barbie! Did you steal her, too?"

"*Ewww*—of course not. I only ever stole one thing besides the baton. . . ." And when he looked at the napkin he was holding, I knew what that one thing was.

"The cookies!" I said. "It was you who put them in the vase."

"Wait—did you guys eat my cookies?" Nate said.

"They were delicious," Tessa said.

Nate sighed. "They looked delicious. I saw them sitting on a tray when I came down to get the baton back. I couldn't resist. But then I had to hide them in a hurry because I heard you guys in the dining room. If you caught me with cookies, I knew you'd tell Mom."

I didn't blame Nate so much for the cookies. But I had a lot more questions. Like why had he tried to get the baton back? One of these days—after I strangled him—I was going to demand answers. But not right now. In the back of my head, I had this feeling I should be able to figure out where the baton was. It's like the pieces were there, but they were jumbled in my brain. All I needed was a quiet place to sit. All I needed was to apply logic. All I needed was—

—to stand in line and greet guests because now they were starting to arrive!

"Young ladies?" It was Aunt Jen. Along with my dad and Granny, she had appeared behind us in the entrance hall. "Take your places please. Nathan? You go ahead."

Go ahead? Where was he going?

There was no time to think about that, though—no time to think about anything. Tessa and I were trapped.

We knew where Hooligan was when he went AWOL. We knew how the cookies got into the vase. But we still hadn't solved the mystery we really cared about.

So, while I ordered my right hand to reach forward, my mouth to smile and my tongue to say, "Hello, and welcome to the White House," I was also thinking about the clues.

What did Astronaut Barbie have to do with the missing baton?

Was there really a White House thief besides Nate?

And then I remembered something else: the two men Tessa and I had seen on Thursday. The ones wearing gray suits.

Who were they, anyway? What could they possibly have to do with the baton?

It is hard to think and be polite at the same time. I said hello to Ms. Nicols, and Mr. Brackbill, the school librarian. Evgenia told me she liked my blue dress, and Alexander reminded me about the tomatoes. Next in line was Courtney. She was wearing a red dress with white dots. I could see why she hated it.

"Hello, and welcome to the White House." I stuck out my hand.

Courtney looked around nervously. "Hooligan's locked up someplace, isn't he? I don't want to be knocked down again."

I couldn't believe Courtney was bringing this up. But I couldn't say anything either. It wouldn't be polite.

Tessa didn't care about polite. "Your dad should leave our dog alone," she said.

"My dad? What's he got to do with it?"

Now I was confused. "He wrote about Hooligan in his blog. Remember? We had a whole fight about it."

"Like I read my dad's blog," Courtney said. "Politics are boring! That fight was about how your dog's a thief."

"No, he's not," I said.

"He stole my marker," Courtney said.

"He stole my ballet shoe," Tessa said.

"Whose side are you on?" I said.

Tessa shrugged. "I'm just sayin'."

And that's when those jumbled pieces came together. "Tessa," I said. "It was Hooligan that stole your ballet shoe?"

Tessa nodded. "The time before the recital. After we searched everyplace, we finally found it. . . ."

Tessa's voice trailed off, and we looked at each other.

"Wait a sec," I said, "did Mr. Bryant say sometimes Hooligan brings him *sticks?*"

CHAPTER TWENTY-ONE

AUNT Jen has told me a thousand times to be polite.

And it's always smart to obey Aunt Jen.

So I looked Courtney in the eye and said, polite as anything, "Would you excuse my sister and me for a moment, please?"

Then I grabbed Tessa's hand, and we bolted.

We were almost to the stairs when Malik blocked our path.

"Sorry, girls," he said. "I'm afraid no one is leaving the state floor for now."

"But it's an emergency! We finally figured out where—"

Malik shook his head and looked stern. I never saw him look that way before. It was sort of scary.

Before I could ask why, Aunt Jen appeared ahead of us on the stairway overlooking the foyer. "May I have your attention please?" Her voice carried above the crowd. "Due to circumstances beyond our control, it appears The Song Boys will not be performing today as scheduled."

What?!

There were gasps, moans and protests. Aunt Jen let the volume drop before she continued. "In addition, I'm afraid I'm going to have to ask everyone to remain where they are for the time being."

"Are you saying we can't leave?" somebody hollered.

In seconds, the mood had changed from glad to angry. And, as calm as she was acting, I could see Aunt Jen was upset. "I'm terribly sorry for the inconvenience," she said. "But I'm hopeful we may soon be able to open the dining room for refreshments."

The word *refreshments* made people perk up. "Why didn't ya say so?" somebody said. The dining room doors were still closed, but a couple of boys moved in that direction.

Aunt Jen seemed to be done talking. I whispered in Tessa's ear, "Granny will tell us what's going on."

We found her discussing *Goodnight Moon* with Mr. Brackbill under the smiling face of President Ronald Reagan—his portrait, I mean. Just like Aunt Jen, Granny was acting all calm, but I could see her eyes were on police alert.

"Excuse me, Mr. Brackbill," I said. "Could Tessa and I borrow our grandmother for just one minute?"

Mr. Brackbill said, "No problem. I was thinking I should head toward the refreshments anyway."

"What is it—what's happening?" I asked Granny when we had her alone.

"And where are The Song Boys?" Tessa asked.

"They're in their bus right outside the gate," Granny said quietly. "But no one's allowed in or out till the security breach is resolved."

"What security breach?" I asked.

Granny looked to make sure no one was listening. "You remember President Alfredo-Chin was here this morning?"

Tessa and I remembered.

"Shortly after he left, he realized his red cell phone was missing," Granny said. "He says it disappeared when he was in the White House, and he thinks someone in our government stole it for the information inside. He's threatening to create an international incident!"

"What's 'international incident'?" said Tessa.

"Very bad news," said Granny.

Tessa looked at me, and I knew what she was thinking. "Cammie—is it possible . . ."

"More than possible," I said. "Granny, we can get that phone back."

"And save The Song Boys!" Tessa added.

"But we have to get upstairs," I said.

Granny looked at Tessa then at me. Her face was solemn, and I could see she was unsure. Then she made a decision. "That's my granddaughters," she said. From her pocket she took a key and pressed it into my hand. "Now act casual."

I said, "Yes, ma'am," and then Tessa and I put dumb, unworried smiles on our faces and sidestepped away.

"Say something ordinary," I told Tessa, and she mumbled, "Something ordinary, something ordinary, something ordinary."

The key Granny had given me was the one you need on the state floor for the elevator. Its entrance is off the hallway in a little room behind a door. When we got to the door, I reached back, turned the knob and then—still mumbling and smiling—I bumped it with my rear end. A moment later, Tessa and I had slipped out of sight.

"Hurry!" Tessa said.

My hand was shaking when I put the key in the lock and turned.

The wait seemed forever.

Finally, the doors opened, and we hustled inside.

Mr. Bryant looked surprised. "Are you sure you girls are supposed to—?"

"Granny let us," I said, and I showed him her key.

Mr. Bryant scratched his head. "Far be it from me to argue with Granny," he said. "Going up."

CHAPTER TWENTY-TWO

WHEN the doors opened, Mr. Bryant said, "Second floor," but Tessa and I were already sprinting. Luckily, Hooligan's bed was empty—and our thieving dog was nowhere in sight.

"Here's the plan," I said. "Piece by piece, we take the bed apart, then—"

But Tessa had a different plan: Grab the bed and flip it. Instantly, a thick cloud of Hooligan hair surrounded us. Not to mention a thick cloud of Hooligan stink—*ewwww!*

After that came the rain of stolen Hooligan treasure—limp brown daffodil petals, hand-lettered place cards, polishing cloth, Courtney's pink marker, a red cell phone . . .

. . . and Colonel Michaels's baton!

I know the cell phone was more important, but I wanted that baton! I reached, but at the same time I heard a dreadful and familiar sound: galloping doggie toenails.

Oh no! I looked up, and there was Hooligan, bounding toward us at top speed.

Tessa and I had the same thought, and we lunged at the same time—*ow!* Our heads collided, knocking us backward. Meanwhile, the sudden move was the perfect spark for an attack of Hooligan frenzy. Before you could say "Stars and Stripes Forever," our dog had his favorite stick in his fearsome jaws and was spinning in the air.

At least he left the red cell phone behind. I pocketed it just as Hooligan turned to face us, cocking his head. Here is what he was thinking: *Nyah, nyah, nyah,* nyah, *nyah!*

In a desperate situation with an excited animal, you should never get all dramatic and yell. Instead, you should move slowly and make soft, soothing noises.

So what did I do?

Got all dramatic and yelled: *"Hooligan!* This is no time to play! This is an emergency!"

And what did Hooligan do? Lunged forward, thumped his front paws, sprang into the air and spun so fast he got blurry.

"Catch him!" Tessa yelled.

And the chase was on.

You can probably picture a too-big dog running fast with a stick in his mouth. And you can probably picture a too-big dog running fast with a stick in his mouth being chased by two girls in party clothes.

Now picture this happening on the second floor of the White House.

Did I mention all the valuable and breakable historic antiques?

We zigged here, we zagged there—and all the time Hooligan's too-long tail was brushing, bumping and rattling anything unlucky enough to be at tail level. We had almost caught up—could almost stretch forward and touch him—when he made a sharp right into the Lincoln Bedroom.

Big mistake, puppy dog! Now we've got you!

Trapped in the farthest corner of the room, Hooligan turned to face us, wagging his tail and slobbering on Colonel Michaels's favorite baton.

Slowly, carefully, we crept toward him.

"Good dog, clever dog," I cooed.

"We'll give you all the biscuits in the box," Tessa murmured.

I was one creep away when suddenly Hooligan thumped his paws and sprang like a jack-in-the-box onto the big four-poster bed. From there it was an easy bedspring bounce right out the door.

Tessa scrambled up and used the bed as a lookout. "Cammie—he's heading downstairs!"

Oh, no.

Downstairs were party guests, the Secret Service, Marine Band musicians, photographers and—worst of all—Aunt Jen!

We had to stop him!

We couldn't stop him.

Soon, we heard the shrieks, thumps and "*Bad dog!*" cries that told us we were too late.

Tessa and I took the stairs two at a time, but when we got to the entrance hall, Hooligan was gone and the scene was like earthquake aftermath. You gotta hand it to Hooligan. He really knows how to make an impact!

Aunt Jen did not look happy.

"Where did he go?" I asked.

She pointed toward the East Room at the exact moment Hooligan ricocheted out—with all my classmates and the Marine Band in pursuit.

It looked like a high-speed parade.

I don't know why Tessa thought of it then—or why we didn't think of it before. But just as Hooligan made a U-turn at the far end of the cross hall, she yodeled: "Hoo-hoo-hooligan—*fetch!*" which caused Hooligan to stop dead in his tracks and drop what he was carrying . . . right in front of Colonel Michaels.

Then he sat back on his haunches, thumped his tail and smiled a big doggie smile, confident he was about to be given the dog yummy he deserved.

Hooligan, I mean. Not Colonel Michaels.

I was out of breath from all that running, but managed to gasp, "Colonel Michaels, look—we got it!"

Colonel Michaels knelt to pick up the object at his feet. But it wasn't his baton at all, it was . . .

. . . Hip-Hop Barbie?

Colonel Michaels stood up again. He was wearing his dress black uniform with gold buttons, gold braid and gold medals everywhere. He was holding Hip-Hop Barbie at arm's length by the hair. I don't think he'd ever held a Barbie before. He looked confused.

Nate ran up. "Actually, I think you wanted this." He handed Colonel Michaels his baton.

Oh, swell. In the end, would Nate the thief take credit?

No.

"All I did was pick it up, sir," he told Colonel Michaels. "Hooligan must've had a spare Barbie down here someplace. When he grabbed her, he dropped the baton. It's Cammie and Tessa who found it. They're the ones you should thank."

Colonel Michaels handed Tessa her Barbie and said thank you. At least, I think it was thank you. I couldn't be sure. His words were nearly drowned out by the sirens.

Oh no—the international incident!

I grabbed the red phone from my pocket, looked around and found Granny. "Here it is!" I yelled.

Granny made a mitt of her hands, and I tossed it. Then she moved faster than I would have thought possible—handoff to Charlotte, to Malik, to Randy—who sprinted through the door.

After a few moments passed, the sirens' wail became a sigh. Seconds later, they were silent.

Coincidence?

I don't think so.

CHAPTER TWENTY-THREE

TESSA and I wanted to brag to everybody: We had solved a mystery! Stopped an international incident! Saved The Song Boys!

We found Dad. He was holding Hooligan by the collar. Hooligan's head was drooping. It takes a while, but eventually he figures out when he's in trouble.

"Guess what—" Tessa started to tell Dad, but Dad wasn't paying attention.

"I want you girls to find a safe place to corral your dog," Dad said. "Safe and escape-proof, I mean."

I took Hooligan's collar. "Okay," I said, "but Dad, Tessa and I—"

"*Now,*" Dad said.

Oh, *fine*.

We took Hooligan to the only person we knew who still liked him—Mr. Bryant.

And after that, things happened fast.

First, Aunt Jen made an announcement. "Due to

changed circumstances, The Song Boys will be performing as planned."

Then somebody—Mr. Brackbill?—shouted, "What about the refreshments?"

"After the performance," said Aunt Jen.

Soon we were shooed into the East Room to take our seats. The Marine Band was already in place—looking snappy in their red and blue dress uniforms.

I sat down and that's when—*finally*—I started to get excited: I was going to see a concert by my favorite band in my very own house!

Jacob Song came out first—he's the oldest—and after that it was pandemonium, everybody screaming . . . then Paul Song appeared, and I screamed loudest of all.

When Matthew came on, he shouted, *"Hello-o-o-o, D.C.!"*

And the audience replied, *"Hello-o-o-o, Song Boys!"*

Then Jacob took the mic. "It's very exciting for three boys from a small town to play the White House—especially backed by the great musicians in the President's Own Marine Band!"

More screaming.

"And we understand that today Colonel Michaels will be keeping the beat because two young detectives found his missing baton! People, give it up for the first kids—Cameron and Tessa Parks!"

Colonel Michaels raised his baton.

More screaming.

But this time it was for Tessa and me!

I felt proud.

And a little embarrassed.

"Now when you people go on home tonight," Jacob Song went on, "I want you all to . . . ." He paused dramatically. Paul played a chord on his guitar. Colonel Michaels brought down the baton, and The Song Boys played a song written just for the occasion: "Read a Book."

In person, The Song Boys were as wonderful as they are in videos.

Only Matt was shorter than I thought.

And Paul had a pimple on his chin.

Besides the music, there was lots of stomping, clapping and screaming. Nate and Aunt Jen danced together. Then Granny and Mr. Brackbill. I started singing along, and Tessa said, *"Shhhh!"* but I ignored her. Near the end, when The Song Boys played "Shake it Up!" the whole audience sang the chorus:

"When life's changin', rearrangin'

"Not to worry—shake it up!"

Finally, with the concert almost over, Colonel Michaels turned toward the audience. Mom had just sneaked in and sat down. I thought he was going to welcome the president of the United States.

That's what usually happens.

But instead, he totally shocked me.

"Madam President, Mr. Parks, ladies and gentlemen," he said. "The Song Boys have asked me to introduce a special guest. Sitting in on piano for our last number . . . the *one*, the *only*, the *first* nephew: *Nathan Leone!*"

Tessa and I looked at each other. So that's why Nate had been practicing so much! Not to mention why he'd been looking for the baton on Thursday!

Our cousin walked up to the stage, nodded to the audience, then took his seat at the piano—all without cracking a smile.

Everybody cheered—even Tessa and me.

Then Colonel Michaels raised the baton, and: "A-one, anna-two, anna one-two-three-*four*. . . ."

The song was Hooligan's favorite, "Rock'n'Roll Dog." From his time-out in the elevator, I could hear him howling along.

Poor Mr. Bryant. Like the music wasn't loud enough.

CHAPTER TWENTY-FOUR

WHEN the concert was over, everybody (like my mother!!!) made a big fuss over Nate.

"What are they going to say when they find out he stole the baton?" I asked Tessa.

"Yeah," she said. "But maybe let's not tell 'em yet—not when people are so happy."

Even I had to admit Nate had played great. Plus once he got started, there was a big smile on his face. Not like our *so superior* cousin at all.

The Song Boys and their dad stayed for the reception. But the Marine Band packed up to go. Before he left, Colonel Michaels called me, Tessa and Nate over.

"Nice job on the piano, young man," he told Nate. "The Marine Band always needs talent. When you're old enough, please give me a call."

"I will, sir," Nate said.

"And as for you, young ladies, I can't thank you

enough. This old baton is important to me, even if it isn't historic."

Nate looked up. "It isn't?"

"Ah, that's right," Colonel Michaels said. "The girls mentioned there was some confusion about this baton and John Philip Sousa's." He told Nate what he'd already told us—how the real Sousa baton is kept locked up.

Nate looked horrified. "Then I made a mistake in my report! Excuse me—I've got to find Ms. Nicols. I sure hope it doesn't affect my grade."

♪♫

The reception was in the State Dining Room. There were three kinds of punch—red, sparkling and blue— and tiny sandwiches on silver trays. No pizza.

Of course my friends were all crowding around The Song Boys. I didn't want to act pushy. I stood by myself and ate a sandwich.

Finally, I saw Nate waving. "Cammie! I'd like you to meet a close personal friend of mine."

Then Nate stepped aside, and there was Paul Song.

Even with a pimple, he was beautiful. He said hi, and I said hi, and he said what a great piano player Nate is, and I said yeah, he really is . . . and then I looked in his eyes and my knees got weak. . . .

So I looked away.

"Oh, no. Not you, too," Paul Song said.

"Not me, too, who?" I said.

"Not you, too, all impressed because I'm Paul some-kinda-big-deal Song," he said. "I figured since you're the president's kid, you'd understand how I'm just normal, too."

"It's not the same thing," I said. "You're super talented. With me, it's just who my mom is."

Paul Song shook his head. "There's loads of people with talent, Cammie. My brothers and I got lucky. And besides, there are times when I do kind of wish I could have my real life back."

Wait—did Paul Song really say that? Sometimes he wants his real life back, too?

"Um . . . sorry to interrupt." Courtney appeared beside us, holding out her program. "Could you maybe sign this?"

Paul took the program. "Who should I make it out to?"

"Um . . . could you just write, 'To my best most gorgeous friend, Courtney Lozana, all my love forever, Paul Song'?" she asked.

"That's kind of a lot," he said, and what he actually wrote was, "To Cortney, Best—Paul Song."

Maybe it was mean, but when I saw he misspelled *C-o-u-r-t-n-e-y*, I grinned. Wanting real life back isn't all Paul Song and I have in common. We're both bad spellers, too.

CHAPTER TWENTY-FIVE

PARTIES are exhausting, aren't they? Especially when you have to chase a rock'n'roll dog.

After all the guests had left, my family—Mom, Dad, Nate, Granny, Tessa and I—crashed in the solarium. Hooligan was there, too, lying on the rug and woofing in his sleep.

Aunt Jen, meanwhile, had gone back to her office for a meeting with Mr. Ross.

The local TV news guys we like best are the ones named Jan and Larry. At 5:30, Dad switched on the TV, and the first thing we saw was Hooligan being chased around the state floor today while Larry's voice said: ". . . in other news, the presidential dog was up to his old tricks, as a White House performance by popular boy band 'The Song Boys' almost had to be canceled."

Then they showed blonde Jan in the studio, shaking her head and looking concerned. "Oh dear, Larry, what did that dog do this time?"

The camera switched to gray-haired Larry. "In

fact, Jan, the incident initially appeared to be serious. It seems the presidential pooch had made off with a phone belonging to the leader of a certain nearby nation. Until the phone could be located, all White House access was curtailed."

Now the TV showed a tall man in a gray suit standing in front of a hotel. A caption in white letters identified him: President Manfred Alfredo-Chin.

"I am a dog lover myself," he told the camera, "so when it was explained to me that the thief was the dog of the president's children, then I understood, and an international incident was averted."

Back to Larry, now smiling. "The foreign leader went on to state that he's pleased to be taking back to his country not only a pledge of support for farms, roads and hospitals but also a unique souvenir of his visit to the United States, a cell phone imprinted with the toothmarks of the presidential dog."

Tessa started whining as soon as Dad hit mute. *"They didn't mention Cammie and me at all!"*

"Sorry, muffin, but we didn't release that part of the story," Mom said.

"How come?" I asked.

"Because they would make a big deal, and you'd be hounded everywhere you went," Dad said. Then he laughed. "Hounded—get it?"

Mom rolled her eyes. "Ha ha. Anyway, the cell phone part I understand. But I do still have some questions."

"So do I." Tessa crossed her arms over her chest,

"Madam President, who were those guys in gray suits on the state floor Thursday—the ones who looked like stupid baton thieves?"

"Gray suits?" Mom was thinking. "Oh—you must mean President Alfredo-Chin's aides. They were doing reconnaissance before his visit." Then—before Tessa could ask—she added, "Reconnaissance means checking the place out. Now is it my turn?"

Tessa said to go ahead, and Mom asked if we could explain how the baton got into Hooligan's bed.

"Hooligan must've found it in one of the East Room fireplaces on Wednesday," I said. "When he did, he dropped the Astronaut Barbie he was carrying and took the baton in trade."

"After that, he brought it to Mr. Bryant in the elevator," Tessa said. "Mr. Bryant's peepers aren't what they used to be—so he thought it was any old stick and let Hooligan keep it."

"Then Hooligan stuck it in his bed—same as he did that time with Tessa's ballet shoe, not to mention the cell phone, the daffodil petals, and all that other stuff," I concluded.

Tessa tapped her head and looked at Granny. "It was all logic, just the way you taught us."

Granny smiled. "You're fast learners. But I'm still confused about one thing. How did the baton get to the East Room fireplace? We already know Hooligan didn't put it there."

Nate had been fidgeting since we started talking. Now I didn't want to look at him. This was it. Time to tell the truth about our *so superior* cousin. Time to send him back to San Diego!

But then I thought how heartbroken he looked when he told us he stole the baton.

And how he gave Tessa and me credit when he returned it to Colonel Michaels.

And didn't he introduce me to his "close personal friend," Paul Song?

Tessa and I looked at each other and, without a word, we came to an agreement.

"Who cares how it got there?" Tessa said. "The point is we found it!"

Nate's jaw dropped he was so astonished. "Wow . . . I didn't expect . . . I mean . . . . *Thanks,*" he finally blurted. But then he shrugged, "The thing is, I already confessed everything to Mom."

"Confessed what?" Dad asked.

"Never mind," Mom said.

"To your *mom?*" Tessa said. "That was brave."

"He's grounded for a month," Aunt Jen said. She was standing at the top of the ramp. She must've just gotten there. "And he has to be extra nice to the two of you, as well."

"*Woot!*" Tessa and I high-fived.

"But right now," Aunt Jen went on, "I need to tell you about my meeting with Mr. Ross. I think it's obvious we can't go on the way we are with this dog. Stealing the odd daffodil is one thing, but what happened today could have been serious. Drastic measures must be taken."

Drastic?

"First of all," Aunt Jen continued, "we have decided to relieve Mr. Bryant of his post in the elevator."

Everybody started to protest: What happened wasn't Mr. Bryant's fault! Plus he had worked in the White House such a long time!

Aunt Jen held up her hand. "We are reassigning him," she said, "to the full-time job of keeping Hooligan out of trouble."

"Oh, thank goodness," Mom said.

"An excellent solution," Dad said.

"Will Mr. Bryant be cleaning the dog bed, too?" Tessa asked.

"That would be a negative," Dad said. "In fact . . . girls? I believe you promised."

"It's Nate's turn," Tessa said.

"*Me!?*" said Nate.

"Aren't you forgetting *nice?*" said Tessa.

"Oh, fine," said Nate. "Where's the stuff I need?"

"We'll show you," Tessa said.

"We'll even help," I said, "but only this once."

Like I said, Hooligan had been dozing. But now, for mysterious doggie reasons, his eyes blinked open.

"Uh-oh," I said. "Don't anybody make a sudden—"

But it was already too late.

AFTERWORD:

JOHN Philip Sousa is known as "the March King" because he composed so many famous marches, including America's official national march, "Stars and Stripes Forever."

Sousa's family lived in the Capitol Hill neighborhood of Washington, D.C., and his father played trombone in the Marine Band. Sousa's first instrument was violin, and he became an apprentice member of the band in 1868 when he was thirteen years old. As a young man, he moved to Philadelphia, but in 1880 he returned to the Marine Band to take over as its director. He had the job for twelve years.

The Marine Band had been founded in 1798, but under Sousa's direction it became more professional and more popular than ever before. When Sousa retired from it in 1892, the baton was presented to him at a farewell concert at the White House. It is embellished with the eagle, globe and anchor emblem of the United States Marine Corps, and engraved with the words: *John Philip Sousa. Presented by Members of the U.S. Marine Band as a token of their respect and esteem.*

John Philip Sousa's successful musical career continued until he died in 1932. Later, his daughters, Jane and Helen, donated the Sousa baton back to the Marine Band. As the fictional Colonel Michaels explains, it is kept in the band's library and used only for special occasions like the change of command ceremony when a new director takes over.

For more on The President's Own United States Marine Corps Band, visit the band online at, www.marineband.usmc.mil.

For more on the White House, including floor plans, photographs and historical information, visit www.whitehousemuseum.org.

I am indebted to Master Gunnery Sergeant D. Michael Ressler, historian of the U.S. Marine Band, for generously sharing his "Historical Perspective on The President's Own U.S. Marine Band, Playing America's Music Since 1798," for showing me the Sousa baton and for his patience in answering my questions. I am also grateful to my friend Elizabeth Bryant Ottarson for giving me a tour of Washington, D.C., providing further details and reading this manuscript. Any errors are, of course, my own.

THE SONG BOYS' GREASTEST HITS

ROCK 'N' ROLL DOG

Music by Charlie Heim
Lyrics by Martha Freeman

Medium Rock

VERSE

As a pup he was-n't much ___ All hang-dog ___ a-nd sad ___

Pa-per train - ing is such a pain ___ and Pup-py chow ___ ta-stes bad ___ Chas-ing

rab-bits was just a bore ___ Fris - bees, ___ who could care? ___ Then he

found him - self ___ a bass gui-tar ___ and gave us - all a scare ___ He was the

CHORUS

Rock Rock Rock Rock Rock 'n' Roll Dog ___ He was an

out - law, fur - ry pawed, bass play - in' dog ___ He was a

laser light, pants tight, rock-'n'-roll dog ___ No more po-ky pup-py Now he loves to rock he was the

Rock Rock Rock Rock Rock 'n' Roll Dog ___ Prac-tice

©2010

Rock 'n' Roll Dog

Rock 'n' Roll Dog

Rock 'n' Roll Dog

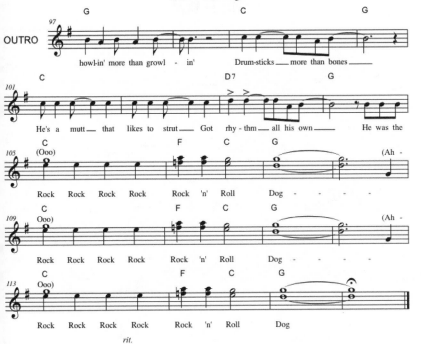

OUTRO

G   C   G

97

howl-in' more than growl - in' Drum-sticks ___ more than bones ___

C   D 7   G

101

He's a mutt ___ that likes to strut ___ Got rhy - thm ___ all his own ___ He was the

C   F C   G   (Ah -

105 (Ooo)

Rock Rock Rock Rock Rock 'n' Roll Dog - - -

C   F C   G   (Ah -

109 Ooo)

Rock Rock Rock Rock Rock 'n' Roll Dog - - -

C   F C   G

113 Ooo)

Rock Rock Rock Rock Rock 'n' Roll Dog

rit.

Read A Book!

Read A Book!

VERSE 2

Lose your-self in the words on the pa - ges   Tell your mom en-thu-si a-sm's con-ta - gious

Tell your teach-er, she sees how you're shrewd-er   What's up with this? Your face just got cu-ter

Read some more and your skills are per-fec - ted   Check it out! That fish is res-ur-rec-ted! You

stash some cash in your sa-vings plan ___ Face it dude, you're one hap-py clam ___ Read a

CHORUS

Book (yes yes, read a book) read a book (yes yes, read a book) read a

book (yes yes, read a book) read a book (yes yes, read a book) read a

book (yes yes, read a book) read a book (yes yes, read a book) read a

book (yes yes, read a book) read a book (yes yes, read a book)

Read A Book!